Kiln Zone

A Mystery

Sharman Badgett-Young

By Sharman Badgett-Young

ISBN-10: 1500194697
ISBN-13: 978-1500194697 (by createspace)

Also available in eBook format from Kindle Direct Publishing.

This is a work of fiction. Characters and places in this story are
fictional or are used in a fictional manner.

Special thanks to my editors,
Jennifer Bardsley
and
Thomas Young
for elevating the quality of this book.

To my mud-families, past and present.

kiln *noun* \ ˈkiln, ˈkil \

[...] an oven, furnace, or heated enclosure used for processing a substance by burning, firing, or drying

Chapter 1

Marca Ruiz rose, smeared in mud from her breasts to her knees—her badge of achievement.

A four-foot urn reared from her potter's wheel. She hugged herself and felt the stretch in fatigued muscles. Bottom to top, she'd pieced together three thrown segments of clay, smoothing the joins until the composite pot appeared as if crafted in a single pull. Since beginning ceramics in college, she'd taken eight years of practice to reach this point. The urn was her masterwork.

She scanned the other potters in the studio, focused on their own creations, and kept her victory dance internal for now, not to disrupt their concentration. But oh, she wanted to crow!

Lisa glanced up under Marca's gaze. "My God, Marca." She circled the wheel. "Wish I could throw like that." Her arm outlined the urn's shape, curving like a belly dancer.

Others rose at Lisa's exclamation, surrounded Marca, and admired the curvaceous pot. At their praise, her feet rebelled, pirouetting an exuberant arc. She grinned till her mouth hurt.

"It's inspired. Only, look at all the clay on your clothes, you poor thing!" Kit, another hand-builder, held a fastidiously assembled coffer in front of her immaculate apron.

Marca tried not to giggle.

The group parted for Dr. Tim French, resident artist, and Dr. Matthew Fyre, Washington State's eminent ceramicist and the leader of this two-week workshop. The friendship between the two men, since Tim was Matthew's student in the 1980's, enabled Tim to set up the class—a coup for Woodsdale's studio of mostly unknown artists. Marca knew that Tim, in his forties, single and childless, saw the potters as a family of choice. She felt the same.

Matthew entwined his fingers, rested them on his stout midriff, and studied Marca's structure. "Masterful. You embraced my process and personalized it. Next week, we'll explore glaze techniques for sizable pieces. Promise me, if your urn is unfinished when I leave, that you'll e-mail a photo when it's complete. I must see what you do with it." He raised his palms.

"I'd love to." Marca beamed, swaying from foot to foot. On impulse, she pinched herself surreptitiously, and giggled when she felt the pressure. *Yep, for real*. It was a heady experience.

She pressed a wire tool tight against the bat and cut beneath her urn. The pot, on its bat, fit on a drying-shelf beside the exit to the kiln area. She swathed it in overlapping sheets of dry-cleaner's plastic. When leather-hard, she'd trim the foot to complement its voluptuous line.

As others cleaned up, she rinsed her drip tray, dumped her slop bucket, and sponged down her wheel. Only Matthew still worked, sorting pieces by dryness for tomorrow's firing.

"See you Monday, mudpeople," Marca called from the door.

* * *

Alone Saturday, Matthew Fyre swung wide the gas kiln's door. Shelves waited just outside it, while those from a previous firing formed a base inside. He hadn't fired this model before, but knew its type. Tapping a button, as a test, he nodded when the cone settings altered.

His shove glided a flatbed cart forward, heavy in his hands. He parked it against the wheel nearest the door where he could reach both it and the greenware needing transport.

Flipping open readers from his shirt pocket, he squinted through them. His notes mirrored his memory—a standard cone 04 bisque for a high-fire clay body. He turned the page.

A footstep sounded behind him. *Good, a helper from the class.* He smiled, but delayed a moment to scan his final notes. Then he straightened, about to turn in welcome.

But an elbow crooked tight around his throat from above and behind. His teeth clipped his tongue. His strong hands, by instinct, flew up to protect his windpipe.

He teetered backwards, tasting blood. A foot jammed into his heels, and stopped his step back to halt his fall. Toppling, he felt himself maneuvered toward the exit.

Five-foot-ten and in his sixties, he was at a disadvantage to this taller assailant. Still, after a life engaged in the physical work of a potter, one known for his massive pieces, Matthew was stronger than average.

He flung out his right hand, trying to seize the doorjamb, as his left continued to pry at the constriction against his throat. He hit a soft object, plastic covered, and then flailed wildly before knocking knuckles against the wall. Twisting his wrist, he scrabbled his fingernails against it, creating a high-pitched scritch as if scraping a blackboard, desperate for a handhold.

Then, viselike, his fingers crimped onto the molding around the door as his foe strained to tug him through it. The ceramicist's grasp slowed the attacker for several moments until his fingers were wrenched free of the doorframe in a jolt of pain, fingernails ripping.

The attacker hauled him outside and Matthew snapped his right hand back to struggle at his throat. His eyes bulged and he battled for air, mouth open like a fish on dry land.

Using his Vietnam training, Matthew altered tactics. He bent his knees into an abrupt squat. The attacker's weight balanced, for the most part, on a single leg after the twist that dislodged the potter's grip. Now, surprise won out. Matthew's weight pulled them down until both were off center.

The arm around his neck loosened, and he sucked sweet air deep into tortured lungs. The two tumbled to the ground, entangled. Matthew pushed the constricting arm up, over, and behind his head in one precise movement.

Shaking free in a jet of energy, he shoved powerful hands against the patio. Exploiting his upward momentum, he leapt ahead, sprinting before he stood upright, fingers pressed together, hands cutting the air at his sides like blades.

Five steps into his flight, a tackle from behind pulled Matthew's legs out from beneath him and knocked him forward onto the ground where his white-haired skull bounced like a coconut against the concrete. Rolling over, dazed, he struggled to focus on his assailant, one knee bending as he used his foot to shove his body backwards, away from the figure. His stomach roiled at the motion of his head.

Matthew gasped aloud. His first glimpse of the visage before him made his skin erupt into goose-flesh. Mouth gaping, the face lunged forward and pulled back as its hands snatched at him, a Halloween ghoul whose features stretched into inhuman lines. A bulky coat masked its body contours, but its lithe counter-movements seemed like those of a person half his age.

He wondered for an instant if a supernatural being had climbed out of hell to suck away his life force. Then he comprehended what his blurry eyes had seen. The features, and the cap of black hair, appeared misshapen because he viewed them through a woman's stocking that the assailant wore over his face.

Matthew pushed himself back again, still too dizzy to stand but scrabbling to stay clear of swinging, muscled arms. His fingers happened upon a chunk of brick behind him on the patio. He hurled it towards the blot of the spook's face above him with all the coordination remaining in his shoulder and arm. Simultaneously, however, the assailant launched a fist at Matthew's head that his instability didn't allow him to block.

The impact vaulted Matthew through fractured light into a dark tunnel that closed in on him, leaving nothing at all.

Chapter 2

Marca spent Saturday at home, catching up on chores set aside in favor of Matthew's ceramics workshop the previous week. But Sunday, as she prepared to attend her weekly book club, she couldn't locate her wallet. She searched the house twice before sitting down to focus her brain on where she left it. Last she recalled, she'd stuffed it inside her pottery locker on Friday.

She hopped in her red Honda Civic and drove to the studio. The view of the Olympic Mountains against the sound couldn't salve her anxiety at having no driver's license along.

Matthew had promised he'd bisque fire every piece he could pack into the kiln. That must mean the majority, if not all of their pots. She'd pick up her wallet and sneak an early peek at the greenware shelf in the same trip.

A studio regular, she used her own key and let herself in through the front door to the ceramics lab. A metallic tang in the air suggested a firing underway.

Her gaze swept the greenware racks. The shelves still looked crowded. *How strange.* Every pot she hoped to decorate remained in the studio, unfired. Her eyebrows wrinkled. *What happened?* She'd have to glaze items she'd thrown and bisque fired prior to the workshop, instead.

Entering the adjoining room, she read the labels on the buckets of liquid glaze Matthew had mixed especially to entice the artists. Turmeric Poppy. Earth in Bloom. Sapphire Satin. The names excited her imagination. *I want these colors on my new pieces, not my old ones.* Her mood chilled further.

She saw Matthew's notebook, open to instructions on firing the gas kiln. Tim and he must have a reason for their altered plans. She took a deep breath and exhaled it, helping herself relax. *If this is the worst that occurs this week, I can compromise.*

Noticing the time, she grabbed her wallet and slammed her locker. The studio door swung closed and she relocked it. She visualized herself replacing her disappointment with anticipation for her meeting, a technique she'd learned years before. No way was she about to let unglazed pottery spoil another moment of her day.

* * *

On Monday morning, Marca arrived at the workshop about a quarter-hour early. Approximately half of the participants had beaten her there and set out their projects on the long wooden tables that stretched across the center of the room, facing the garden view out the wall of windows. She figured that, like her, they valued each minute of Matthew's instruction, and didn't want to miss even a casual suggestion from the master before class began.

"Greetings mudpeople," she called out. Voices echoed in return.

Lisa hugged her. "Gotta do this now. I'm not going to hug you later, if you're all squishy again." She grinned. "I have my limits, mudwoman."

Lisa built by hand using a decorative knack that Marca envied. Unicorns, rendered in under-glaze, rampaged across the pentagonal box she had constructed for her niece. They looked real—or would if unicorns weren't imaginary. To keep it out of the clay, Lisa wore her light-brown hair pulled back, revealing a porcelain complexion. Lisa's beauty exuded from inside and out. However, hand building didn't jacket the younger woman with wet slip. Marca viewed herself the luckier of the two.

Marca laughed. "I bet it all started during childhood. Maybe my mother didn't let me stomp enough puddles or decorate my mud pies. So now I make up for all the fun I missed by taking my clay baths."

"Oh, you. So deprived." Lisa gave her a playful shove and they chuckled together.

"Were your pieces in the bisque fire this weekend?" Marca asked. "None of mine made it. I checked on Sunday when I stopped by and rescued my wallet from my locker."

"Let's open up the kiln and find out."

"You go ahead. I'm dying to check on my baby." Marca nodded at her draped urn.

With a mother's gentleness, she removed the sheet of plastic she had wound around its top and inhaled the after-rain earthiness. She laid her palm against its cool surface and tested the resistance of the rim. Later today it would reach the perfect texture for trimming.

She removed the remaining plastic, and her eyes were assaulted by an indentation the size of an apple that dominated its base. She let out a low, "Ohh." Knuckle marks, distinct in the moist clay, showed where someone had struck the pot a sharp blow.

"Hey," she said, louder than she planned. "Look at this gouge. Does anyone know how it happened?" She directed the curious eyes of the potters to the depression with a sweep of her forearm.

Several murmured empathically, having experienced unexpected damage to wet pieces in the past. But everyone seemed clueless about whose fist had marred the urn.

"You're lucky you threw it recently. The blow would have destroyed a drier pot. I bet you can flatten it out," Kit said, "so no one notices."

Marca scrutinized the imprint. "You're right, it's reparable. I'm just shocked by the damage. But I can reach inside with a paddle and slap out the indentation." Skillful repair would leave, at worst, a slight irregularity.

Still, it irked her that nobody confessed. Of course, the person may not have arrived yet, and an apology might ensue at any time. She harrumphed once to herself then consciously let go of her anger, unwilling to give it power over her.

"Oh no!" At the cry, Marca turned to see Lisa rush back into the studio. "The kiln is empty," she said. "Not one pot inside. And there's this inexplicable mound of sand on the bottom. It's uncanny."

Curious, Marca, Kit and the two Korean-American potters followed Lisa out to the sheltered kiln area. For over a decade, the gas kiln had served as the studio's workhorse. The status window indicated its last function—a firing that started Saturday morning and completed at the atypical temperature of cone 02.

The substance lay in a roughly crescent-moon shape on the base of the kiln where pots usually sat stacked for bisque firing. Marca picked up a pinch of the gray granules and felt coarse, sand-like grit when she rubbed her finger and thumb together. It didn't feel like clay at all. She doubted it would dissolve in water. The pile of sand spread the length of the shelf, heaped higher towards its center. She sniffed, but perceived no scent except the dust that inevitably collected in the shelter.

A flutter of disquiet crept into her stomach. *Something sinister happened here.* She looked at Lisa, who frowned. She imagined her friend felt the same.

"Where is Matthew?" asked Lisa, looking around the kiln shelter as if he might step out of the wall like a genie from a lamp. "It's time for the workshop."

"Past time." Marca nodded at the kiln's timer. "I bet he's inside by now. Let's check the studio."

All members had arrived and set up for the day, resuming work on their projects. Matthew was not there. The only men Marca saw were the two male studio members.

A grandfather, Dave Miller, improved his throwing skills every week. He owned his own wheel and kiln at home, but joined the studio for the companionship. His tee shirt, not covered with clay slip, showed a man holding a pot and read: *My wheels are for throwing.*

Burly Quentin Brenner, several years Marca's senior, had the sweet features of a younger man. His stilted gait, however, revealed side effects of long-term psychotropic medication.

Tim dashed into the room. "Sorry I'm late, everyone. Hope you started without me." His head swung around as he inspected the room. "Where's Matthew?"

Heads shook negatively, and a few voices sounded I-don't-knows. Eyes flicked up to the clock before returning to projects underway. Matthew, who had come in early each day during week one, was already fifteen minutes late.

The familiar routine did nothing to alleviate the queasiness in Marca's belly. It increased incrementally as she wedged her clay, filled a bucket with water, and organized her tools at one of the wheels. She surveyed the studio. Other than Lisa, nobody acted as disturbed as she felt. But then, the studio always radiated focused relaxation—a shelter from the craziness of the outside world.

"So, nothing got fired," Ju-Mie, the older Korean-American woman, said to Marca as she paused from shaping a set of dishes at a neighboring wheel.

Marca said, "No. Yet the kiln ran through a full firing cycle. It's very odd."

"Should I sweep out the kiln?" Lisa asked in a low voice, leaning down toward Marca. "We need to load a bisque before we leave today, since nothing got fired over the weekend. I'd rather use the large kiln, considering how much work is crowding the shelves." She pointed her chin at the greenware.

"No, not yet," said Marca, not quite sure why she opposed Lisa's offer. "I'll take a couple of photos first. With Matthew running so late, things feel off kilter today. If I have some pics, I'll have an easier time explaining what happened when I describe it to others, later." She rinsed her hands in her bucket and dried them on her pants, leaving muddy streaks she didn't seem to notice, and then took her cellphone from her pocket.

Lisa looked relieved. "I think something's wacko, too. I'd feel better if we documented the firing, just in case. Unless Tim knows what happened." The friends' eyes met, and together they went looking for Tim.

The slight man spoke on his office phone, frowning. "You mean, even though his room was unused since the cleaning service arrived on Saturday morning, you didn't think to call anyone." Tim paused, listening. "I've heard that before, too, but I think it's an urban myth. There's no waiting period before you can file a missing person report. Doesn't the well-being of your customers concern you?" He paused again. "Yes, I suppose confidentiality is also important." His scowl seemed to indicate the comparative weight he gave it.

"Well then, I'll call his wife in Spokane and see if she knows anything. If I find out more, I'll get back to you."

Ending the call, he rubbed his eyes with the heels of his hands. "This is alarming. Nobody has seen Matthew since Friday evening. The motel says his bed hasn't been slept in since Friday night."

"He vanished," Marca said.

"Seems that way," Tim said. "Hold on, though. There's one more call that might clear up the mystery."

The women remained in the office instead of offering Tim privacy as they usually did. But Marca sensed they were bound together in this potential catastrophe. Perhaps Tim felt the same, because he beckoned for the two women to sit.

His next call intensified Marca's dismay. Although she couldn't make out the words, she heard the volume of Alice Fyre's voice increase as the call progressed. Alice, 16 years Matthew's junior, had been married to him for over 20 years.

Tim hung up.

"She last spoke to her husband Friday evening and was unaware that anything was amiss before my call."

He took in a deep breath and then rubbed his face with both hands. "I don't know what to think. This is very unlike Matthew."

"That's not all that's strange, Tim. Saturday's firing was messed up in a major way. You have to come out to the kiln," said Lisa. "We need your insight on something weird inside it that I discovered this morning."

After the coolness of the dark office, the bright sunshine made Marca squint. Summer weather had nearly arrived in Puget Sound. A cool Pacific Northwest breeze flowed past them as they walked toward the kiln shelter.

Lisa pointed out the peculiar settings and the kiln, nearly empty. "I tried to figure out what happened, but only managed to rule out a few possibilities. That matter's not clay or powdered kiln wash, and there's a scad of it. Nobody had a pot large enough to disintegrate into a pile that huge. And if a pot did explode, we'd see larger shards in a smaller pattern. Do you recognize this stuff?"

"Not offhand," Tim said. "Give me a minute here." He knelt by the control panel to the kiln and pulled up several mini-screens of reports on the weekend firing. "Cone 02? Matthew planned a normal bisque fire to cone 04 this weekend. Cone 06 to 04 makes sense for high-fire clay in a bisque, but 02 to 1 matures low-fire clays like earthenware. This firing doesn't fit the clay body he chose for us to use in his workshop."

"Maybe he made a mistake," Lisa said.

"Matthew knew his cone settings by heart back when I was in his class decades ago. And near the back door, I saw his notebook open to the page he wrote while we discussed the kiln and the firings that we planned. Considering his experience, and that he even consulted his notes, there is zero possibility that Matthew misfired this kiln. But somebody did—someone who didn't understand much about ceramics."

The women hazarded no opinions. Marca felt as confused as Tim sounded. So, while Tim took notes on the firing, Marca photographed everything, including the screens of information and Tim studying them.

Finished reading kiln screens, Tim stepped to the open door and knelt to rub a pinch of the grainy substance between his fingers just as Marca had. He confirmed the women's suspicions that, not only was it neither kiln wash nor clay, it wasn't any chemical he kept on hand for glaze formulation either. He sprinkled the material onto the palm of his hand and examined it closely, but had no more idea what it was than they had. He put a small bit on his tongue, and then spat it out into his hand, where he mixed the saliva and sand together. It didn't dissolve.

"My best guess is that it's sand. But where was it gathered?" he asked. "There's no taste of salt which I'd expect if the sand came from a Puget Sound beach. In fact, it had no taste at all. It's irregular, with larger bits mixed in—stone chips perhaps. Nothing like what we find near the ferry."

"This is all too weird. We better call the police," Marca said.

"Yeah, you're right. We better bring in a professional," Tim said, nodding agreement. "Matthew is missing, a dozen of you paid a hefty price for his instruction, and this firing was irregular. The whole muddle makes no sense to me."

* * *

Officer Benjamin Mulback arrived about an hour later. The potters had spread out around the studio, building by hand, throwing or decorating their ware. The tranquil ambiance the studio usually held was absent, however.

Everyone seemed to wait for something, Marca thought, although she admitted to herself that they might simply be waiting for Matthew's call with a plausible excuse for his nonappearance. She knew better than to let her emotions run wild, but they kept fighting to take her over.

Tim led the officer into his office, and the two women followed.

"Please, tell me everything you know about Matthew's absence," the middle-aged Benjamin said as they sat down. He took his hat off his light brown hair, and set it aside. "Do you mind if I record this interview?"

The three potters shared what they had discovered about Matthew's disappearance—the unconventional firing, his notebook, and Tim's conversations with the potter's distressed wife and the motel manager. Benjamin jotted notes as they talked, in addition to his recording. Then he asked for the names and phone numbers of the studio potters, and Tim printed out a class list for him.

Marca mentioned the damage to her pot that she discovered that morning. "I can't imagine how it connects, except that it happened since I went home for the weekend. It could have occurred Friday evening, yesterday, or even this morning, though nobody admitted they knew about it."

Benjamin asked to see the kiln. Near the back door, he paused to examine Matthew's notebook, still spread on the table near the greenware shelves, and studied the urn briefly, jotting another terse note. He was thorough, and didn't dismiss the fist-print, but Marca saw from his manner that the damaged pot didn't excite him.

When they reached the Kiln, Benjamin's gaze first turned to the control panel that Tim indicated. He showed the same amount of interest as he had with the urn. But when he looked inside the kiln, Marca saw his eyes open wide. He squatted down and studied the grey substance without disturbing it.

He took out a tape measure from his pocket, and measured the length and width of the pile.

Then, he removed a jeweler's loop, and gazed at the grains under magnification for several minutes, scanning different sections of the sandy heap. He asked about the spots where the substance had been touched, and Tim and Marca admitted that the pinch marks were theirs. After another minute, Benjamin put his tape and the loop back into his pocket, his face inscrutable, and rose to his feet with an aura of command that Marca hadn't noticed until that moment.

He made eye contact with each of the three potters in a deliberate way that demanded attention. "I want you to leave here. Immediately. Don't touch anything—you could destroy evidence. Try not to step on any footprints on your way out.

"I no longer consider this a missing person report. It is officially a homicide investigation. I must secure the crime scene."

"Why, what is that stuff in the kiln?" Marca asked, the sick feeling from her stomach trying to climb up the back of her throat.

"I can't be certain, but I can offer an educated guess," Benjamin said. "The substance in the kiln appears to be human cremains."

Tim's eyes opened round. He gagged once and grimaced. He dashed from the kiln shelter and spat into the dirt where a strip of garden had been planted. Ignoring Benjamin's order to touch nothing, he turned on the hose, rinsed his mouth and spat again. And again.

Chapter 3

Benjamin Mulback not only required the kiln, patio and back door blocked off, he demanded evacuation of the entire studio building immediately, via the front door. "Do not put away your tools or wash the tables or wheels. Leave everything where it is except for the purses and coats that came in with you this morning. Show those to me on your way out so I can catalog them. Touch nothing else, walk nowhere but out the front door, and don't enter the restrooms or use Tim's computer or phone."

"Sorry about the calls I made this morning," Tim said.

"I understand. You didn't realize that a crime took place here. Please don't reenter your office now, however. Have you turned on your computer and signed in on your e-mail account this morning?"

"Yes, first thing. I checked to see whether Matthew sent me an explanation about his absence, but there was nothing."

"That's fine. Leave it running. The evidence people will shut down the computer for you when they finish in there."

"Hey, can you please allow the potters who worked on pieces today to cover them with plastic before they leave? That's how we preserve them from drying out," Tim said. "Otherwise, their work will be ruined by the time they return."

After a brief discussion, Benjamin assented.

As Marca picked up the first sheet of plastic to cover her creation, the officer said, "Not that piece. It is evidence. Please back away."

"But she was covered in plastic when I arrived this morning. And she will be spoiled if she dries like this." Her voice wavered.

"Are those the plastic sheets you removed from your pot this morning?" he asked, pointing to the one in her hand and the other lying next to the pot. "If so, please do not handle them further. The crime scene team needs to bag them and take them into custody for analysis as evidence."

Obediently, she set down the plastic sheet. But seeing her week's triumph about to be compromised, Marca broke into tears. "I put my heart into this workshop, and what I've produced is valuable to me. Please let me wrap fresh plastic around the urn. She is my finest work of art—larger and with more potential than anything else I've done. I can't bear to see her harmed," she sobbed. "Please?"

Benjamin paused, studying Marca and her urn. Then he pulled fresh plastic from a bin. After donning disposable gloves, he re-wrapped the pot as Marca instructed, carefully keeping plastic from touching clay surfaces, except for the pot's rim. He tucked the clear sheet beneath the bottom of the bat upon which the urn sat.

Then, Marca was swept out of the studio through the front door just like all the other potters.

* * *

Detective Anders Johanson, striding straight and thin, arrived next, his light skin a startling contrast to his dark businessman's suit. As chief investigator, he nodded his head as he reviewed Benjamin's notes. The scene was secure, interviews complete, and Benjamin had scrupulously followed procedure. His sketched map indicated the evidence found on his walk through. Although physically unable to isolate the potters, he asked them not to speak to each other. They waited, scattered about on the front sidewalk and lawn.

In his early 30's, and five years into his career with the Woodsdale Police Department, Anders was still teased about being the new guy at the P.D. rather than a seasoned detective. He worked each case diligently, knowing that recognition in his profession came only with achievement. Still, he was ready for his indoctrination phase to be over.

This was the first time he'd been called in as chief investigator on a homicide. Woodsdale crimes were mostly thefts and driving infractions. Serious, non-domestic attacks against individuals were rare.

This case may prove my value to the department. He tried to push that thought out of his mind as he donned sterile booties, plastic gloves and a hair cap. Distraction wouldn't improve his technique.

After checking for dust footprints, he walked through the crime scene, referring to Benjamin's entries and searching out missed details to include. Next to each piece of evidence unmarked by Benjamin he placed a numbered marker that referred to the list he would turn over to the crime scene investigator. He took stills and video, even though he knew the previous officer had done the same. Redundancy meant thoroughness in an investigation.

He inspected all parts of the building, the patio, and the fenced-in kiln shelter. He made a checkmark by each numbered sign Benjamin had listed of a struggle outside the back door. A pair of reading glasses lay broken on the concrete patio. A stain near them appeared to be blood. What looked like a human hair stuck to the blood. A faint footprint showed where a worn spot in the patio surface had allowed dirt to collect.

Anders believed in the investigative process. He made every effort to learn what he could, first from the scene and Benjamin's notations, and then from those closest to the situation. He had the resident artist provide a list of everyone who had contacted Matthew since he was first invited to lead the workshop. It included several board members of the Woodsdale Arts Commission. Anders attached the list to the report—people he would contact.

The criminalist, Mrs. Ana Nguyen, whom Anders knew was top notch, arrived with her assistant. A pencil thin skirt with a slit up the back, and razor-spiked heels, made Ana, who was naturally petite, appear nearly five-foot-four. He understood that she had started out as a police officer before realizing she had a special flair for crime scene investigation. He wondered how she dressed back then.

The two women stood just outside the front door while they covered up their street clothes with paper gowns in powder blue. Ana slipped off her heels, pulled on paper trousers, tucking her skirt inside them, and swapped her heels for athletic shoes she'd brought along in a canvas bag. Then both tucked their hair beneath elastic-edged caps, put on goggles, pulled booties over their shoes, and tugged on latex gloves, all in powder blue, before they stepped inside using studied precaution.

"You are the height of fashion as always," Anders said to Ana, ten or twelve years his senior. He let his gaze travel over her one-size-fits-all over-garb. "Simply mouth-watering. Especially the cap."

"Are you willing to make good on that compliment?" she asked. She batted her eyes at him through her cerulean goggles. Her eyes were the only things left that weren't blue.

He grinned at her comeback. Their playfulness made the mundane parts of the investigative process more tolerable.

Wasting no time, she began an inward spiral to research, record, photograph, and bag the evidence. Her assistant swung into action as well. They taped shut each bag after labeling it in detail.

"Benjamin writes that there's a wet, plastic-wrapped pot that we need as evidence. Apparently it's the *magnum opus* of one of the potters. Anything you can do to protect it is appreciated."

"I'll do my best, handsome."

"Thanks. I know you will, beautiful."

Taking off his own cap and booties, he left the studio and interviewed the potters, comparing their statements to those they gave Benjamin, probing for a bit more. The impact of the crime on them was obvious. Some seemed shocked, while others appeared anxious to escape from the scene.

A couple of the potters were shaken by the crime. One was Quentin. Anders suggested the potter talk with a counselor if the stress didn't pass.

Murder was a devastating event that changed how people looked at their own lives. They lost, not only the person killed, but a protective sense of personal invulnerability as they came face-to-face with mortality. Death was no gentle teacher.

He photographed the bottoms of their shoes, noted what they wore, and jotted down their vehicle makes, models and license plate numbers before he released them. Tire tracks, shoe prints and trace evidence might remain in the parking lot that could tell more of the story, so he asked the studio members not to re-enter it to retrieve their cars until tomorrow evening. That should give Ana time to examine it. They obeyed, a few calling taxis while the rest car-pooled home with friends who had parked on the street.

Anders chewed the inside of his cheek. On the surface, he heard little of significance from anyone except the three primary witnesses, Marca, Lisa, and Tim. But Benjamin's notes contained a suspicion about Quentin, who "described himself as mentally ill, an odd thing to say to an officer."

Anders resolved to visit Quentin at home and complete a more thorough assessment of the man. He might prove to be their first suspect, unless Alice Fyre lacked proof that she had remained in Spokane throughout the weekend. The spouse was nearly always the initial suspect in a murder investigation.

Back inside the studio, the criminalist and her assistant progressed meticulously through the crime scene.

"I'm off to canvass the neighborhood, babe—knock on doors—but I promise I'll check in with you before I leave for the day. Got to see that pretty face one more time."

She smiled at him and curtsied, as if the paper gown was a courtly robe and she the queen.

As he traveled down the street, he asked people what they saw and heard on Saturday. He felt a momentary flash of hope as he questioned the barista at the Starbuck's across the street from the lab, because he had worked his shift at the time the fight must have taken place. But the man offered nothing that would help the homicide investigation. Many houses stood empty, but the people he met, some of whom sincerely wished to help, also had no news about the pottery studio over the weekend.

"They're pretty quiet over there," a woman in her 80's told him with a shrug. "All the wild stuff goes on at Starbucks."

"Can you give me an example of something wild you've seen there, ma'am?"

"Well, a balding man, with grey hair pulled into a pony tail, like a girl, goes in there every day." She attempted a demonstration, pulling back her shorter locks. "Perhaps he's the owner, but he's one of those hippies. You know them: sex, drugs and rock and roll." She gave him a sage nod.

"Thank you for your help, ma'am," he said, displaying a serious demeanor that he found challenging to maintain. *A hotbed of hippy crime at Starbucks. Nothing like the mere murder across the street.*

He heard his voice run a repetitive loop as he moved from one home to the next. *Blah, blah, blah.* But he followed procedure to the letter. He distributed business cards and asked interviewees to call him if they remembered details later. He mentioned he would swing through the neighborhood again another day. In the end, however, he doubted his canvass would yield any leads.

He trudged back to the pottery lab and peeked inside at a moment when Ana, with her back to him, bent over to scrape at a spot on the floor.

"Ah, you even share your best feature with me," he chuckled.

Ana stood up and glared at him, her cheeks, pink from bending low, mimicking a blush of embarrassment she didn't seem to feel.

"I'll look forward to your report," he said. "Looks like you have quite a few goodies to offer me."

"Lots to sort through," said Ana, ignoring the double entendre. "We'll need fingerprints from the potters to see if any we pulled are unexpected. If you get DNA cheek-swabs and hair samples from them as well, you will guarantee that I'm a happy babe."

"Always my goal, sweet thing," he said. "I'll have Tim and Marca spread the word. Let me know who doesn't come in within the next day or so, and I'll prompt them. I'm heading back to the office now."

"So it goes with you guys. Love us and leave us." She flashed him a long face. Her assistant grinned.

* * *

Marca darted from one task to another, completing none of them, her scattered mind unable to stay focused. So much had changed since she awakened early this morning. Memories—Matthew, the studio, the cremains, Lisa, Tim, her urn, Detective Johanson and Officer Mulback—flew about in her head like moths. They would neither alight nor fly in any organized formation. *If I wore my hair long, I'd pull it out, but pulling short hair simply isn't dramatic enough.*

She brewed a mug of Earl Gray and then drew a hot bath, determined to regain her sense of control. While the tub filled, she lit a candle and meditated on the mandala that hung on her living room wall. She could usually find a pool of calm within it.

But her one family photo from childhood pulled her gaze away, and for now, she turned its face to the wall. She no longer welcomed the drama from her early life, and she intended all she had learned during years of counseling to support her, now and in future instances of uncertainty as well.

To be honest, however, she found that today's murder challenged that equanimity. In fact, she caught herself hyperventilating as she bent to turn off the tap, and had to sit on the toilet seat while she concentrated on breathing normally. *I'm glad nobody saw that.*

She climbed into the tub and sipped her tea. The warm infusion soothed her throat while the rose scented bath oil soaked into her pores. She closed her eyes and leaned back against her inflatable wine bottle pillow. Her arms made snaky motions in the water, encouraging her muscles to let go of the knots they'd formed over the past several hours. A soft moan escaped her lips as she felt the heat begin to melt away her tension. She relaxed like that for ten minutes or more, feeling more herself as time passed.

At last, she opened her eyes and finished her now tepid tea. As her anxiety had decreased, the images in her mind settled into order, and she flicked through the events of the day like a slide show, able to be more objective.

A memory of the cart, parked between the wheels and the greenware shelves, came to her; she hadn't thought of it until now. It stood outside on Friday, beside the kiln, but inside when she had stopped in on Sunday. *Is that important?*

Anders had encouraged the workshop participants to call with any additional details that might affect the investigation. So, once she got out of the tub and dressed, she retrieved his business card. She felt slightly embarrassed about reporting such a minor detail, but dialed his number anyway.

"Am I disturbing you?" she asked.

"Not at all. I was just tying on my running shoes."

She explained about the cart. "I figure you know whether that's important or not. But you asked us to call."

"Thank you, Marca. I did. I'll check that the crime scene investigators covered the cart thoroughly.

"By the way, I'd like to visit you tomorrow, at your convenience. I have some additional questions you could help me with."

"Fine," she said. "With the workshop canceled, I have loads of free time. Oh, uh, now that I'm rested and more myself, I'm sorry I reacted so strongly about my pot. After all, Matthew is dead. That's far more important."

"I appreciate the apology. But I also get it about the pot. I could tell from what you said that you'd made a breakthrough."

"You had enough to do without dealing with some crazy woman and her urn. I must have seemed totally self-absorbed. But I'm not the type of person who uses tears to get my way. I want you to know that."

He laughed. "Don't worry, I didn't think you were. Let's talk some more tomorrow. Is 10:00 a.m. okay?"

No longer embarrassed, Marca found herself smiling as she hung up the phone, still hearing his laugher echo in her mind.

* * *

The detective hit the pavement. Running was the perfect catalyst for making sense of the jigsaw puzzle of evidence as it collected in an investigation. Exercise helped him clarify his sense of the case.

He headed down 68th Ave. toward Woodsdale Community College. He pondered Alice Fyre. As the younger, second wife to Matthew, he wondered about her desire to take advantage of his years of investments toward retirement. Wouldn't be the first younger wife to do so.

Before Marca's call he had spoken with Alice. Executive director of a NGO—a non-governmental organization—that streamlined services available to local people in need, she spoke freely from her private office. She had progressed from concocting scenarios about her husband's disappearance—ones that resolved into happy endings—to "what ifs" in case worse news should arrive. She answered Anders's questions in detail, grasping each one as if it was the life preserver that would rescue her Matthew from drowning.

Without realizing it, she gave him an alibi for Saturday—she had been with friends in Spokane all day. Anders checked it out and it seemed valid, though it meant nothing if she hired someone else to take him out. His instincts told him she was innocent of complicity in the case, though he needed to keep her under observation until the case resolved. But the authenticity of her emotional pain was difficult to question. *Unless she was experiencing second thoughts.*

He reached the college, where a path looped around an adjoining golf course. Turning onto it, he felt the friendlier cushion of bark chips beneath his feet.

He had not mentioned the remains found in the kiln to Alice yet, despite his assumption that they were her husband's. The connection between Matthew's disappearance and the discovery of the cremains was circumstantial, since they took place the same weekend in a similar place. But until he received an analysis of the ashes, he wanted to protect her from the additional pain an incorrect hypothesis would cause. For all he knew, the remains belonged to a large dog, and her husband was alive somewhere.

He let the rhythmic thud of his feet on the trail fill his consciousness for several minutes, allowing space for whatever might filter up inside himself. Eventually, he reached the end of the unpaved path and turned back onto the sidewalk that led towards his house.

He had hoped for new inspiration during this run. Instead, his expectation remained unchanged—that the granules found in the kiln would prove to be Matthew's remains. A more satisfying resolution seemed unlikely.

A wave of unexpected weakness washed over him as he imagined the next call he would make to Alice. He was not looking forward to it. Time was slipping past like the distance beneath his feet. Doors of opportunity were closing. The announcement of Matthew's death was imminent, he was sure. Because even if Matthew had not yet perished, the likelihood of finding him alive had already plummeted.

Chapter 4

Marca opened the door to Detective Johanson at 10:00 sharp the next morning. She invited the detective off the quiet street and into her cozy three-bedroom rambler.

She watched the detective take a leisurely glance around the living room. It was decorated with framed wine bottle labels against watermark backgrounds of vineyards, tasting rooms, or wineries. The shape of bottles, sketched around their labels, gave a three-dimensional sense to the artwork. The glazes on her pottery accented the colors on her walls from the shelves where she chose to display them. A wine bottle on the dining table held a dry arrangement she had gathered of wild teasels, Indian tobacco and wheat.

She felt buoyed by his attention to her artwork, and had to grin. *Great to have someone take an interest.* "Please, have a seat," she said aloud.

He flashed her a smile. "Thanks."

"So, how goes the investigation? Did the stuff in the kiln turn out to be—," Marca crinkled up her nose as if smelling moldy waste, "cremains?"

The detective gave an easy laugh, a sound she already loved to hear. "I thought I was supposed to ask the questions."

"Oh, right. Sorry. The murder's been on my mind. I can't stop thinking about it. It's the first time I've been so close to a serious crime."

"I can imagine. Did you know Matthew Fyre well?"

"I was beginning to. Increasing the size of the pots I threw was my main goal in the workshop, and he helped me improve. He gave everyone personal help—drew out our talents. But before the workshop, I had never met him."

"I have your statements, but I'd like to know more about Matthew, the studio, and the other potters, if you don't mind. The more clearly I can recreate the studio in my mind, before the murder occurred, the better able I am to see connections that otherwise might escape me."

She described the workshop for him, but shuddered at the memory of the gritty substance on the floor of the kiln. "That's really creepy. Somebody had to shove him in the kiln, latch it, and coldheartedly turn it on, right?"

"So it seems, if those are indeed human cremains. Whether they were Matthew's or not will need research as well."

"I didn't think of that. But who else's might they be? And why? Is anyone else missing from around here?"

"Exactly the questions we need answered as well. And here's another. Who, besides the potters taking his workshop and its organizers, knew that Matthew would be alone at the studio on Saturday?"

"Yes, I wondered about that, too. Tim gave you a list, right? There may be people involved that the potters don't know. Members of the artistic board might have helped set up the details of Matthew's travel. Maybe he shared his schedule with them."

"How many people, besides the potters, have you seen around the studio over the past month or two?"

"The studio always feels like it belongs to us. Few strangers come inside—I don't remember any since, oh, maybe the Christmas season. See, it's our sanctuary, a creative refuge that we depend on. Suddenly, it's full of frightening images and death. That spoils the serenity, and I hate that."

"Tell me this," the detective said. "Who might want to harm Matthew? Did anyone argue with him? Was he critical of somebody's work? Has he mentioned having enemies? We have no motive for murder yet."

"I don't know. He's famous, but only in our limited art realm. Not the kind of person who draws media attention to himself very often. His pieces bring in good money, of course, but he's no Bill Gates."

"So none of the potters were upset with him."

"Our potters? Oh no, no. Everyone learned a lot. We enjoyed his confidence in our abilities. He helped us get past blocks that held us back in our craft by using humor and inspirational stories. He was a gifted teacher. The workshop was a wonderful opportunity for all of us."

"Did he say or do anything that seemed unusual, especially toward the end of the week? Or did he seem preoccupied or worried?"

"Not that I noticed. He never mentioned family or business troubles. But again, check with Tim. Their friendship is why Matthew agreed to come at all. Groups like ours can't usually afford the fees charged by an award-winning specialist like Matthew Fyre.

"For me, Matthew's one-on-one instruction finally moved me past a learning plateau that limited the size of my pieces," Marca said. "I want my hobby to support me, at least partially. I'd rather be at the studio than on my computer. My urn symbolized success in that pursuit, but I realize now that my future can't be made or broken on a single pot."

"I appreciate your understanding. We attempt not to harm the items we take into custody as evidence, but wet clay is awfully fragile, and we need to run tests on it. I can't promise you will get to finish the pot, or even get it back."

"Okay. Thanks for letting me know," Marca said. "But I've found my peace about the urn. If she helps solve the case, I'm glad to donate her."

"What work do you do on the computer?"

She gestured to the winery pieces on her walls. "I design logos and marketing art for the wine industry, half time. These are some of my labels."

"I admired them when I came in. Didn't realize you had created those as well as the pots. You have a pleasing grasp of color and shape."

She giggled and squeezed her toes inside her shoes. "Thanks. I'm ecstatic when a new line of wine takes off. I like to believe that my art improves the flavor just a smidge." She held up her thumb and forefinger about half an inch apart, and saw him smile.

"You see how this investigation goes then. My work is mainly asking countless questions and chasing down answers that lead to new queries." He smiled. "I have a long way to go. Give me a call any time. I appreciate your information about the cart. And if you think of anything else—?"

"I'll be sure and call," she said.

"Oh, by the way, I plan to stop in to see Quentin Brenner later. What's your take on him?"

"He has been a studio member longer than I have. It's therapy for him. I think he's on disability or something, for mental health issues. And from what he says, he still lives at home with his parents."

"Excellent. Thanks for the tip."

"Once you get him talking, he'll share everything he remembers. He's a little quiet at first, but he's a sweetie. His mother works not far from the studio, so she drops him off on her way to work. He doesn't drive."

"Have you seen him get angry before? Or does his illness ever make him violent?" Anders asked.

"Quent? No way. I can't even picture it. In fact, I can't imagine any of the potters being violent.

"These are good people who like to relax together in artistic flow—sort of a mindful bunch, if you can understand that. I'm probably the most volatile of the group, but I've never hurt anyone."

"It's hard to imagine violence by people we care about," he said, his vocal pattern indicating to Marca that his visit was about over.

"You don't suspect he killed Matthew, do you? Was there evidence—fingerprints or something—that made you ask about that?"

"No, no. It's more of an initial interview."

"Like visiting me."

"Yes, something like that. No worries." He rose to leave.

"Oh, okay. Get ahold of his parents then. I bet all three will want to help you, if they can. We all will." She held the door for him as he stepped onto her front porch.

"Thanks again, Marca. I enjoyed seeing your artwork. I hope we get a chance to talk again soon."

Marca watched the blond detective's long confident strides to his car, and gave a wave as he climbed inside. *Me too. Definitely.*

* * *

Anders picked up a framed photo from his tidy desk and smiled at the faces of the kids on the baseball team it displayed. His office was typical of those detectives were assigned—private so that they could talk about sensitive matters on the phone, but small—just large enough to individualize with a few items that expressed their personality.

The framed photo reminded him of another that he had recently received via email. Setting it down, he rifled through his inbox, and found a head and shoulders shot of Matthew Fyre that Alice, Matthew's wife, had supplied. With a piece of tape, he affixed it to the wall above his desk. He studied the face of the victim. *I'm going to catch whoever did this to you, I promise.*

He felt some discomfort about his conversation with Marca. True, interviews with all the potters were mostly for clues or bits of information that would further the case. But murder by stranger was comparatively rare. Persons close to the situation who knew the victims often turned out to be the murderers. He planned to assess any information that might indicate such a link. Of course, that would be true with Marca as well, if evidence suggested she was a suspect.

Yet Benjamin had requested he check out the unusual conversation with Quentin. It was a bit more than a routine interview, but only a trifle. He shrugged. *It's not that different.* He was professional in his interviews. But he wanted to be especially authentic with Marca, who seemed so open with him. He didn't want to behave in a way that might disappoint her.

He dialed Quentin's number.

"I remember you," Quent said.

"May I come over and ask you some more questions? I'd like your folks to be there, or at least one of them."

"Yeah. That's okay. I'll leave a message for my dad. He gets home first."

"Great. Have him call me, okay? Do you still have my card?"

"Uh, let me see. I think I put it in my pocket yesterday," Quent said. He was gone for a minute, then said, "Which officer are you? Mulback or Johanson?"

"Johanson," he repeated.

"Okay. I remember you. I'll have him call," Quent said.

"Thanks Quentin. I hope to see you later," Anders said.

* * *

Anders stood in the morgue, his nose twitching at the putrid scent that the air conditioner never seemed to banish. He swiped menthol Chapstick under his nose.

Minutes before, he'd received a call that the medical examiner was about to do the post-mortem on the suspected cremains from the kiln. Despite his distaste for autopsies, he had run down the stairs, too intrigued to wait for the elevator. He saw that his boss, the chief of police, had come to watch the autopsy as well.

The room was large and open, with sterile-white walls, polished metal, and a gray cement floor. To Anders, it looked like a mix of a hospital laboratory and a locker room—especially with the drains in the cement floor. His eyes skipped over the drawers where cadavers were stored, and focused on Ana Nguyen instead.

She attended as per protocol. Ana probably had the most work of anyone during the first couple days of an investigation. Yet, despite her long hours, she looked energized—ready for another day of solving puzzles. Her touch of makeup accentuated healthy skin, full lips, and deep brown eyes.

A compact marvel. He shook his head in admiration. Her face turned toward him, and she raised her eyebrows. The corner of his mouth turned up, and he winked in response. She gave a faint smile as she looked back toward the medical examiner.

The M.E. wore a white lab coat over his street clothing and a matching cap. Set before him on the table, in place of a body for autopsy, was a plastic bag filled with the substance Ana had collected as evidence. He pulled on sterile gloves, turned on a recorder and described aloud his process.

"These are the official notes of Medical Examiner Michael Cleaver in regards to an autopsy of a suspected homicide victim, case #20140607-1. In the absence of an identifiable corpse, this is a visual analysis of suspected cremated remains, also called cremains, vacuumed into a sterile evidence bag from the investigatory scene. Evidence suggests that the victim may have been incinerated during the firing of a Woodsdale Studio kiln where the cremains were discovered.

"I also have before me a photograph of the suspected cremains, showing the position in which they were found, along with measurements of the length and width of their distribution. They formed a rough curve, vaguely similar to a person lying on his or her side with knees drawn up partway.

"This is one possible position a body might assume during cremation, out of many. Likely, tendons would constrict during the incinerating process and pull the limbs of the deceased in toward the body core, away from their original position in the oven. The photo of the substance inside the kiln shows us nothing conclusive about the distribution of the remains." The M.E. set the photo aside.

"The weight of the substance is—," he paused to place the bag on the scale and move the counter weights back and forth for an accurate measure, "7.87 pounds, a weight similar to the average for remains, after cremation, of an adult human male.

"However, please note that bone is the main contributor to the weight of cremains. Adipose tissue, skin, muscle and liquids vaporize, adding no weight. The primary difference, therefore, between the weight of male and female remains is due to men growing taller, on average, than women and contributing more bone. The body of a tall woman could also have generated these cremains, or an animal with a similar bone mass.

"I will now sift the substance several times using sieves of decreasing sizes, and place the resulting divisions of particles into separate sterile containers." Again, the M.E. paused while he completed the actions, which took him about ten minutes.

First he poured about one-half cup of the substance from the evidence bag into the sieve with the smallest screen, and shook it with a back and forth motion until material stopped falling into his first receptacle. He dumped the remaining material from the finest sieve to a medium sieve, tapping several times to make sure nothing remained caught in the first screen before he repeated the sieving. He then moved on to a large screened sieve. All particles remaining in the largest sieve he poured into a fourth receptacle. He continued the process, one-half cup at a time, until he emptied the evidence bag.

He tipped each receptacle from side to side, inspecting its contents. The first three siftings were fairly uniform in appearance. He described the differences in size from one sifting to the next. When he reached the final receptacle, he spilled out the remaining several pounds of contents into a large, low-sided aluminum pan about 1.5 by 2.5 feet, and tipped it gently to spread the material in the thinnest layer possible. He set down the pan as he reached for his microphone.

Anders heard Ana gasp when she saw what lay inside.

Chapter 5

Marca had taken the week off from her work in order to attend the workshop. Now she felt ambivalent about how to spend her unexpected free time. With the murder investigation ongoing, she was too preoccupied to produce her best electronic artistry, though she had computer work waiting.

She had begun reading a new horror book, something that provided a bit of the adrenaline rush she identified with home, growing up. Usually, that gave her enough of a thrill that she didn't need to act out as she had with her family.

But today, she was already antsy and didn't need more excitement. What she needed was activity. *Something constructive to work out my über-drive.*

She got out the stepstool and dusted the tops of bookcases. She moved furniture to clean underneath, as much to feel the flex of her muscles as because it was actually necessary.

As she jerked her couch back into place, she thought of the other potters enrolled in the workshop. Many probably felt a similar disorientation to hers.

They displayed varied specialties in the studio, but one thing they did well together was eat.

Suddenly certain of her purpose, she decided to hold a potluck at her house, and invite the studio members to attend on Friday. With all the effort she was expending, her house would be clean and inviting for her guests.

"In addition to the food, bring clay if you want to hand-build while we visit," she told each one. "I don't have many flat surfaces, so bring a cutting board or lap desk if you can. We'll make the space work out."

The response was positive. Battling the limbo of the unfinished workshop, the potters yearned for an opportunity to discuss the tragedy together. *An opportunity to heal.*

Her heart lightened now that she anticipated hosting her friends. She twirled a circle and clapped her hands twice above her head. Then, grinning, she scoured her kitchen spotless.

* * *

Anders, partially blocked by the police chief, stretched up on tiptoes, straining for a glimpse of whatever caused Ana's exclamation. In the bottom of the pan, a glint of gold caught his attention. He glanced up at Cleaver. Visually unperturbed, the M.E. picked up a pair of forceps, and spoke into the microphone again.

"The first item I remove, from the coarsest collection of particles left after sifting, appears to be made of gold. It is a band in a large size that might be described as a man's ring, though that is not definitive, as finger size can vary greatly, especially in an obese person. As I turn the band in the light, I see a smooth exterior surface, with no sign that a setting was once attached."

He turned the ring back and forth several times. "There is an inscription inside. It reads: 'Love as long as a ring is round.' I am placing the ring into an evidence bag of its own, sealing it with tape, and labeling it."

Anders watched as he did this.

"There are additional pieces of metal in the tray, probably medical in nature, such as screws from a broken bone needing special support. Some may have come from dental work such as amalgam fillings, bridgework, or crowns. They also go into an evidence bag and receive tape and a label.

"Finally, I'll remove the largest pieces from the remaining debris, bone by appearance, and place them into a separate evidence bag which I will label. Note that the pieces are fragile, disintegrating at slight pressure from the forceps. The criminalist attending this autopsy may wish to route these samples to a facility where DNA testing can be attempted."

He stirred the remaining material in the bottom of the pan in small, overlapping circles using his forceps, working from one end of the pan to the other so as not to miss any particles of interest. He extracted nothing else from the remains.

"I will seal the remaining material from each sieving into a separate bag for further analysis, as requested. Mrs. Nguyen, will you please sign for receipt of the evidence containers now?"

She stepped forward with her pen, and then collected the small box of evidence packets from the M.E.

"This completes my autopsy. Thank you to those who attended." He punched a button that stopped the recorder.

As Ana left the morgue with her box, Anders caught up to her. "Hey, Ana. As soon as you verify what those metal fragments are, let me know, would you my dear? That could support or contradict our theory that the cremains are human before we receive results of the DNA testing."

She gave him a slow grin. "I suppose I could do you that favor, handsome."

"Thanks. I already owe you."

"Oh, I haven't forgotten, magic man. The day will come when I ask you to pay up, you know. Your pretty face won't keep you off my hook forever."

"That's my girl," he said.

She punched his bicep.

* * *

After the autopsy, Anders called Alice Fyre. Once a deceased person was identified, the P.D. informed the immediate family as quickly as possible. It wasn't an easy task, but for the sake of loved ones, it was important.

This situation differed, since little existed by which the body could be identified, and the metallic and DNA analyses had not been completed. However, a DNA test on cremated bone was often inconclusive, and the extended time at extreme heat during a firing would make decipherable DNA even less likely.

Considering the wedding ring the M.E. had found, and his supposition that the metal pieces in the evidence bag had medical and dental sources, the hypothesis that Matthew Fyre had been immolated in the kiln appeared more convincing. The remains hadn't come from an animal, certainly. He felt duty-bound to let Alice know that he suspected her husband had been cremated alive.

"Alice, since we spoke yesterday, I have come up with some additional questions I need to ask. I also have some information to share. We located a man's wedding ring with an inscription inside. Did your husband wear a ring?"

She caught her breath. "Yes. He took it off when he threw to protect the gold from the sandpaper grit in the clay, but he always kept it with him. All these years I worried that he would lose it, taking it off like that, but he never did."

"Can you tell me if it was inscribed?"

"I had these words carved inside, 'Love as long as a ring is round.' It had personal meaning—a phrase we used to whisper to each other in the early days, before we married. Where did you find it?"

"I'm afraid we found it in remains cremated inside a kiln during a firing at the studio where Matthew led his workshop. Although we still have tests to run, initial findings point to those being your husband's remains. I'm sorry."

He heard what sounded like a muffled sob, followed by a long pause. He waited, his eyes moistening for her.

"Excuse me," she said at last, a tremor in her voice.

"No problem. I know this must be difficult to hear."

"He was inside the kiln when it was fired? How could that happen?"

"We are investigating, but we suspect he was murdered. There is evidence of a struggle nearby."

"Who would murder my sweet man?" Her voice slid higher in pitch.

"We don't know yet. Have you thought of anyone who disliked or was upset with Matthew?"

"No. Everybody appreciated him. He won awards, not just for his ceramics, but for his exceptional teaching ability, too. You should see the cards, photos, and other memorabilia his students presented to him over the years. And he volunteered at the hospital in Spokane, helping people needing occupational and physical therapy, teaching them ceramics. He even has loyal friends from when he served in Vietnam—men whose lives he saved." Her voice became strident as she spoke.

"It sounds like people learn much more from him than ceramics. Please excuse my question about hard feelings people may have had towards him. Similar questions have helped close cases in the past." Anders kept his voice gentle.

"I must lie down. I don't feel well at all. Is there anything else?"

"We need his medical and dental records released to us so that we can compare them to the remains. But you don't need to do that at this moment. Rest first. Get back to me when you feel stronger."

"Thank you. I'll do that, detective. Goodbye." He heard the sound of a handset missing its cradle at first, then, with a scraping sound, sliding home.

* * *

Anders proceeded through his calls and visits to both those involved in the hiring of Matthew Fyre for the workshop and to the potters themselves. Because of Tim's relationship with the deceased, Anders felt particularly drawn to him as a source of information. He had not dismissed the man as innocent, although his alibi for Saturday was strong. And nobody had observed anything but friendliness between the two men. *He could have contracted the killing.*

Like the other potters, Tim appeared to have no motive to kill Matthew. Statistically though, other than Alice, Tim was the most likely suspect, and Anders expected to conduct several thorough interviews with the man as the case progressed. He looked forward to the summary of the information taken off of Tim's computer.

* * *

Later in the afternoon, Mr. Brenner returned Anders's call, and scheduled a meeting for that evening at 5:00 p.m. When he arrived, Anders found both Quentin's parents at home.

"Quentin, did you have a chance to fill your parents in about Matthew Fyre's disappearance?" he asked.

"It sounded, from what Quent said, like he was murdered, and his ashes found in the kiln," Mr. Brenner said.

"That is our working theory. Certainly somebody's cremains were found, and Matthew is missing."

"That's such a shame. He was making a special effort with Quent," Mrs. Brenner said. "So many people don't bother."

"He showed me how to center clay in a new way. I've never been great at it, but my pots were looking better," the potter said.

"Sounds like you got along with Matthew, Quentin," Anders said.

"Quent. I go by Quent."

"Pardon me. Quent then."

"Yeah. He was awesome. I liked him a lot. It's really sad that someone killed him. Do you think you'll find the bad guy?"

"That's what I'm working on, Quent. I'll do my best."

"We are concerned about Quent's protection," Mr. Brenner said. "How safe will the studio be when it reopens?"

"Several potters have asked about that. Of course it's a concern. But if the doors are kept locked, I think it should be safe inside."

He turned to Quent. "But it's important that you keep your eyes open and report anything unusual you see, okay? Everybody needs to be eyes and ears for the others. And if you're waiting for a ride, wait inside the locked door."

"Okay."

"Quent, did you ever argue with Matthew, or have any reason to be angry with him?" Anders asked.

"No, I don't get angry very much. Only if people mock me or try to take advantage of my disability. And then I talk it out with Mom and Dad." His eyes flicked to Anders's and away several times as he spoke.

"Does that happen often?" Anders asked.

"No," Quent said.

"Quent is a gentle young man, and quite responsible. He just needs some help in living," Mrs. Brenner said.

"So no episodes of violence?" asked Anders.

"No." Quent rocked from foot to foot.

"Not even before he was on medication," his mother said. Her voice sounded artificially polite, and she pressed her lips together, as if trying not to frown.

"Can I ask you something, detective?" Mr. Brenner asked.

"Of course. Go ahead."

"Did you ask the other potters about their violent tendencies when you interviewed them?"

"Now that you ask, I didn't. I only asked if they argued or knew of anyone else who was upset with Matthew."

"So enlighten me. What evidence requires you to treat Quent like this—differently from all the other potters?"

"None," Anders said, "The reporting officer suggested in his notes that I find out why Quent mentioned his mental illness in his initial statement, I'm following up. I hope you'll excuse any questions that seem unnecessary. I'm doing my part in assuring a thorough investigation."

"He shouldn't suspect me of killing Matthew just because I have a mental illness." Quent said, his voice a little louder. "I've met lots of people like me who never hurt anyone." His eyes shifted to Anders and away again. To and away. To and away.

"Well, I don't believe that, though my questions probably sounded that way. I'm sorry if I upset you, Quent."

"People see that I'm different and they get uncomfortable—try to blame things on me. It's happened before. I never hurt anyone, not even when I was a kid, or when I used to hear voices in my head."

"From my experience," Anders said, "people assume killers must be mentally ill because they killed someone—which is quite different from the few people with mental illness diagnoses who commit murders. Overall, it's not much different than the rate of people as a whole who murder."

"I told the other officer about my mental illness, because I'm not ashamed of it. Sometimes it makes things easier if people know. That's all." To and away. To and away went his eyes. The strain in his voice was clear to Anders.

"Do you have any other questions, detective? If not, it may be time for us to get dinner ready," Mrs. Brenner said, her voice cool.

"I'm finished for now. Don't let me hold up your dinner. But if I have more questions in the future, may I call again?"

"Yes. As long as Mr. Brenner or I attend whenever you talk to Quent."

"Of course."

Chapter 6

After leaving the Brenner's home, Anders called Marca. Her voice on the phone sounded more relaxed than it had the day before.

"By the way, what should I call you?" she asked. "Detective?"

"Well, if you don't mind me calling you Marca, you may call me Anders."

"Anders. Thanks. What's up?"

"I attended an autopsy on the cremains since I talked to you. Lab tests will help us determine if they are Matthew's remains or not. But there is nothing in the weight, composition or distribution inside the kiln to make us doubt it."

"Such a shame." He heard her sigh.

"I know. That's why I do this work. No one should get away with robbing a person of their life."

"I agree.

"Hey, I wanted to tell you that I've arranged a potluck at my place for the potters on Friday. I know they'd appreciate an update on the case then, if possible."

"Good idea to keep them in the loop. Something I share might bring up a piece of the puzzle that they didn't realize they held. Tell you what. Why don't I stop by again on Thursday and let you know what I've discovered."

"Cool. I'd appreciate that. Besides, I like seeing you."

Her words surprised him, but in a pleasant way. On impulse, he said, "Ditto," and laughed.

After he bid her goodbye and went to pick up dinner, she kept surfacing in his mind at odd moments. Every time she did, he smiled. He couldn't help it. It made him shake his head and smile again.

Anders knew the rules. No way was he allowed to date a potential suspect, and for good reason. But something about Marca intrigued him. Maybe her joie de vivre. *She makes for a fine view, too.*

* * *

Wednesday morning, Anders smiled when he saw that Ana Nguyen had left a message on his office voicemail. He called her back.

"What news my dear?"

"What's it worth to you, pretty boy?"

"Oh, so now you're going to manipulate me with the promise of information?" He grinned to himself.

"Who's talking about information?"

"Don't tempt me," he said.

"Okay—your choice," she said in a flip tone. He heard papers rustle, and then she continued in her professional voice.

"Our first tests on the cremains came back negative—no DNA information. Considering that they came from a kiln, I'm not surprised. Phosphodiester bonds are the glue that holds DNA nucleotides together. Extreme heat destroys those bonds; so cremated remains often have no DNA left.

"However, bone fragments the size of those I received for testing may not have received the intensity or duration of heat needed to totally decompose the DNA. If we're lucky, a piece may have been partially sheltered, or in an area where air intake kept the kiln from firing to temperature. It's a long shot, though."

"So we're out of luck then?"

"Inconclusive tests are a poor sign, but there are more sensitive ones we can run. Don't give up hope yet. We may still identify the DNA. But we're certain to learn more when we receive the medical and dental records from Alice Fyre. We can compare them with the metal found in the cremains. Even without a DNA match, we'll have more certainty about the victim's identity after that."

"I'll look forward to hearing what you find, assuming the price is reasonable, honey bun."

"I'll make sure it is, turtle dove. Here's some better news. While going through the e-mail copied from Tim French's studio computer, a tech found that Matthew Fyre mentioned the amount of his life insurance policy to Tim at one point—said that he was insured for two million dollars. You might ask Alice if he talked about the amount openly. Seems odd that he shared it with his friend."

"Interesting. A potential motive—the first we've found—and for one of the people closest to the deceased. That's definitely worth further investigation."

"Other than that, he found no sign of any suspicious electronic interactions between the two men. Their relationship seemed mutually supportive, their conversations authentic. I have copies of the e-mails for your review in case you see something we missed."

"I'll look through them. But the insurance policy is exactly what we hoped to find. Thanks, Ana."

"Just wish we'd had more telling results from the DNA lab for you," she said.

"I know you'll do your mojo on the evidence from the crime scene," he said. "If anyone can identify those remains, you can. I appreciate your expertise."

"You young fellows lay it on thick, I've noticed." She laughed.

"I try to."

"Keep it up, babe, I like it."

* * *

Wednesday morning, Anders found a voicemail on his phone from the guard assigned to watch the pottery studio.

"Peter Landsbury here. Somebody came by the studio early this morning and tried to open the front door. I was walking rounds toward the back of the building when I heard him, so I started back his direction, keeping out of sight. The crime tape is evident around the building, and it crisscrosses the doorway, so the sound of someone rattling the knob was suspicious.

"By the time I got to the front, all I saw was a bulky male form vanishing into the Starbucks across the street. Whether or not the Starbucks fellow is the same man, I can't be certain, but I suspect he is.

"I didn't hear a car, so I think the fellow arrived and left on foot. And I didn't see anyone else in the area. I would have heard running if he took off.

"Tomorrow I'm off work, but I'll leave a note for Roy Tenison, who'll be my sub. I'll ask him to stay close to the front of the structure tomorrow, out of sight, in case this guy returns. I'd like to know what he was up to."

Anders called the officer back.

"Have you touched that knob since you heard it being turned?"

"No sir. I didn't know if you'd want to lift prints off of it."

"Good man. I'll have Ana send someone over."

* * *

Alice Fyre arrived in Woodsdale that afternoon with red eyes and uncombed auburn hair that made her look closer to her age than usual. She went straight to the Woodsdale Travel Inn where her husband had been staying, and checked into his room. Achy from the four-hour drive, she accepted the bellhop's offer to carry her suitcase upstairs for her.

When she reached the room, a torrent of emotion cascaded through her body. She stopped outside the door, hand half-extended toward the knob, frozen.

After a pause, the bellhop reached for her keycard. "May I help you with the door ma'am?"

She snatched it away from him reflexively, then, seeing the astonishment on his face, said, "It's alright. I can get it."

She slid the keycard into the lock and pushed the door open, suddenly wanting the interminable moment at the threshold to be over, just as much as she had feared it ending a moment earlier.

Inside, the room looked clean and the bed had been made. She saw Matthew's suitcase against the wall, plus a pen and a few coins on the small table, but little else that indicated that the room had been occupied. She let her shoulders fall from where she had carried them, squashed up nearly to her ears.

Noticing the bellboy standing just inside the door, she fumbled through her purse. Handing him a tip, she stepped toward him to hurry him out and then closed the door behind him.

Once alone, Alice walked about the room, touching random objects, her mind a blank. She opened the closet, and saw his clothes. They sat in neat piles on the shelves with other miscellaneous items he had brought along.

She opened his suitcase next, and set it on the bed, but found little inside: mints, a few papers, a notepad. She left the bathroom for last, imagining his razor, toothbrush and toothpaste, and his comb, sitting lined up beside each other, next to the sink, like he kept them at home. But when she stepped inside, only the toothpaste and a bottle of his Lisinopril tablets for high blood pressure sat by the sink.

In a panic, she searched every surface of the bathroom, tossing aside the carefully folded towels in her haste. She tried the mirror to see if a medicine cabinet hid behind. But nothing else of Matthew's turned up. The towels and paper-covered drinking glasses had all been replaced since his stay.

She picked up her phone and called downstairs. A receptionist answered.

"I need to speak to the manager right away. I believe there has been a theft from my room," Alice said, her voice trembling.

The manager came on the phone immediately. "What seems to be the problem, Mrs. Fyre?"

"Some of my husband's things have been removed from his room without my permission."

"Please excuse me, ma'am, but at the request of the Woodsdale Police Department, I allowed a crime scene specialist to come in and collect the items that might provide evidence for the case. I believe she dusted for his fingerprints and took away items that might contain DNA to compare to the scene of the crime, including some dirty clothing, the sheets, and a few personal items from the bathroom.

"I should have told you immediately, and I apologize. I got involved in my work, and didn't notice when you arrived. Also, let me express how sad we all are, here at the Travel Inn, to hear of your loss. Matthew seemed like a fine man."

"Oh. Thank you. Of course. I should have figured that out." She said the expected things to get the manager off the phone as soon as she could.

The absence of her husband's toiletries hurt—a personal violation. Missing them, all aligned in the bathroom, felt like missing out on a final glimpse of Matthew himself. The enormity of it took her breath away. She wouldn't even get to lie in the sheets where he had spent his final night.

She shook out and refolded the clothes from the closet, all that remained of those Matthew had brought for his two-week stay. She raised each item of clothing to her nose, and inhaled deeply, before she folded it, trying to catch his unique scent. All she smelled was detergent. They were unworn. His scent had been stolen from her, too.

She packed them into his suitcase, taking her time, recalling how he looked wearing each outfit. Her heart weighed at least fifty pounds.

She packed away his other scant belongings from the closet and bathroom as well, her eyes tearing up at the missing toothbrush and comb. Under his shirts, she found outlines for the second week of the workshop, and a set of handouts he had prepared. These, she set aside to give to the detective.

The quick nap she laid down to take somehow lasted until dinnertime. She had planned to visit Officer Johanson during the afternoon, but even after her rest, she was overcome with weariness. The four-hour drive, the stress of finding Matthew's belongings missing, and her grief had exhausted her. She ordered food from room service, and it arrived in about 10 minutes. She had already forgotten what she requested by the time it was delivered.

Turning from the door with the dinner tray, she noticed their wedding photo on the table beside the bed. *Oh my Matthew.* She clunked down the tray, picked up the picture in both hands, sat on the bed he had slept in, and wept, inconsolable. *My sweetheart—I hope I told you how much I loved you the last time we spoke. Love as long as a ring is round.*

Chapter 7

In the morning, Anders checked for messages. Officer Roy Tenison, substituting for Peter Landsbury—guarding the pottery lab—had called 15 minutes before.

"That big guy was here again today, the one Landsbury said he saw enter Starbucks yesterday. He tried the front doorknob of the studio, and then left when he found it locked. I took a picture of him with my cellphone, but I didn't interrupt him. I'll forward it to your cell. Looks to me like a major suspect just surfaced."

Curious, Anders took out his cellphone and called up the photo. Roy had gotten a good likeness of the face. As soon as he saw the photo he recognized the man. It was Quentin Brenner. *This is unexpected. Just what are you up to, Quent?*

But Alice interrupted his thoughts before he could follow them further. She showed up in a salmon-colored, pleated pantsuit that accented her feminine figure and touches of makeup that brought out the sculpted lines of a model's face--despite the red eyes she could not mask. *What an oddly matched couple she and Matthew would be.*

She stood at Anders' office door with copies of her husband's medical and dental files clutched to her chest. Anders rose, turning his attention to her.

"Alice, welcome. I'm so glad you got here safely. Was the pass clear?" While he spoke, he took the files she thrust at him and laid them on his desk. Then he extended an arm to shake her hand. But she ignored his polite overture.

"What have you found out about Matthew's murderer?" she asked, grasping both his upper arms. She stared into Anders's eyes as if they held salvation deep inside.

He cleared his throat. "I wish I could tell you that the case is solved, but it's still early in the investigation. We've found few leads yet to help us identify a suspect as our murderer."

He glanced at her hands, firmly cuffing his arms, and struggled inside himself for the right words to say. When he looked into her eyes, the emotion in them was raw enough to push his gaze back to her hands. He touched her elbows.

"I'm still knocking doors, interviewing people with alibis, and awaiting lab results. But the records you brought should help enormously. They'll allow us to certify the identity of the remains."

Still staring at him, Alice's face gradually morphed from an artist's study on petition into lines of resolve. She dropped his arms and pulled herself up straighter. Her role of executive director showed in her stance.

"I want copies of every lab report on the crime scene that you've gotten back so far. Since I knew Matthew better than anyone, something might occur to me that others missed. I'll take them with me now, so I can read through them this afternoon."

"An excellent thought and appreciated. I expect more reports before the end of the day. I'll have the receptionist make copies for you of what I have now. Then, before I go home tonight, I'll copy anything new that comes across my desk and leave it in an envelope at the front counter for you to pick up in the morning.

"By chance, did your husband have medical plates or screws in his body from past surgeries?"

"Yes, he broke his leg in a fall from a ladder five or six years ago, when he was putting up Christmas lights on the house. It necessitated a plate to hold the bone in place while it knit together. Luckily, it healed well. He considered having the plate removed but never took time off for the procedure. Seemed like it didn't bother him that much, unless we were going through the metal detector at the airport. Is that important?"

"It could be. We'll comb these reports for clues to help identify the remains. Did your husband have a life insurance policy?"

"Yes, for two million dollars. I told him I thought that was extravagant, but he said he wanted to be certain I would be comfortable if anything happened to him. I can tell you, I've never been so uncomfortable in my life. Money seems meaningless— dry and sterile—when I try to compare it to our marriage."

"Who else knew about the policy?"

"Our lawyer and the financial advisor, of course. I have no idea how many others. Matthew might have talked about it with someone else and not thought to tell me. But I don't believe I mentioned it to anyone."

"Tim French apparently knew about the policy. Your husband told him in an e-mail we found on his lab computer."

"I wasn't aware of that. It does seem odd, but they were close friends. I know he trusted Tim."

"Money is a common motive for murder."

"I suppose so, from the movies I've seen. And yet, when it happens to you, it is hard to imagine. The idea makes me ill." Her mouth twisted.

"I can't guess yet whether it was a factor or not. At this point, it's important to follow all possible leads."

"Do whatever you have to do, detective. But promise me that you will find my husband's killer. I don't want him doing this to anyone ever, ever again."

"That's my goal, every minute of this case. I'll do my best. And you, Alice, I know you had a long drive yesterday. I hope you're settled in as much as possible while the process moves forward. Where are you staying?"

"In Matthew's room at the Woodsdale Travel Inn. Someone needed to collect his belongings, and we paid ahead for the room, anyway, through Friday night."

"Oh yes. That makes sense."

"I'll give you the address and phone number. I have my cellphone with me as well. If one number doesn't work, try me on the other. I want to know the moment you find out anything about Matthew."

* * *

As the dinner hour approached, Anders found himself thinking about Marca again. He would be stopping by her place in a little over an hour to share information with her for the potters coming to tomorrow's potluck. He looked forward to seeing her again. After Alice's distress, Marca's joy would be a balm.

He filed away the reports on his desk, shut down his computer, and considered where he might pick up a little food before the meeting. There was a taqueria between the police department and Marca's house that he enjoyed. It was quick—halfway between fast food and sit-down fare—one of those order-at-the-counter places that didn't serve your food in plastic. He had just enough time before he met with Marca to eat there.

* * *

The dark-haired man slipped past the crime scene tape and surveyed the patio where he had defeated Matthew Fyre. He smiled. *The old fart gave a better fight than I expected. Made for a very entertaining morning.*

He was careful not to disturb anything as he gloated over the scene of his triumph. He'd proven he was the alpha wolf. *This is my territory now. Fyre never had a chance.*

* * *

Marca, driving home from the post office after mailing a birthday card to her mother, looked at her watch. She had just enough time to grab a bite before Anders came over. She pulled in at a place not far from home.

She stepped up to the counter, already knowing what to order. As she turned away, number in hand for her order, she saw Anders enter the front door. Her hand flew up to smooth her hair, and she realized her mouth was open. She closed it just before he met her eyes with a start of his own.

"Well, this is a happy coincidence," he said breaking into a smile. "May I join you at your table?" He seemed relaxed and pleased to see her.

"Of course," Marca giggled. She chose a table by the window, and watched Anders place his order at the counter. She liked what she saw. His full white-blond hair and blue eyes were startling, even here in the Pacific NW where skin saw little sun. They clearly revealed his Scandinavian heritage.

She had dressed up just a notch this morning, and added a touch of makeup, wanting to look attractive for him when he arrived at her place this evening but without being obvious. Now she was glad she hadn't waited until the last minute.

He slipped his wallet into his pocket and brought his number over to her table. He pulled out his chair.

"What a surprise," she said.

As always, he laughed easily. "A pleasant one," he replied. "Hey, let me grab us a couple glasses of water. I'll be right back."

He walked across the room to the water dispenser. She watched him in motion. *Pleasant indeed.*

"Here you go," he said, setting the glasses on the table. He pulled up his pant legs as he sat, then scooted his chair up to the table. He sat across from her: light against her rich Latino coloring.

"Is this unusual, having dinner with somebody you know through a crime investigation?" she asked.

"A bit, I have to admit. But while I wouldn't have set it up this way, perhaps it was meant to be." He ticked off his points on his fingers, a self-effacing smile on his face. "I get to talk with a major witness in a relaxing setting. Discussing the case before your potluck saves me from briefing the potters myself. And I have to eat sometime." He laughed again.

"Don't worry, I'm not complaining. Just seeing if I'm as lucky as I suspect." She let loose a laugh as well, one that trickled like water over stones, and her toes danced intricate little patterns under the table.

"I'll take that as a compliment," he said with a grin.

She grinned back.

"I didn't know you liked Mexican food. This place may have a limited takeout menu, but it's as authentic as it gets. My mother makes tacos using her family's recipe whenever I visit her. These remind me of hers, which is saying something."

"I have favorite dishes I grew up with as well. I have yet to find a restaurant that gets them right, though. My mother is proud of that. She entices me to visit home by tempting me with food." He laughed. "There's nothing like family, is there?"

"No, but that isn't always saying something positive. My father was not an admirable man, I'm afraid—an alcoholic who deserted us. But our lives improved after he left. The rest of us drew closer. We're a demonstrative group, overly dramatic, I suppose, but loving. And we stand up for one another."

"I'm sorry about your father. Are you still in touch?"

"Not for the past ten years, and frankly, I'm relieved. My mother hears from him occasionally. He asks for money, or shelter from someone who's after him for money—always mistakenly, as he tells it. His behavior would only drag me down. I choose to be a positive person, and I have plenty to be thankful for. I do just fine with my remaining family and close friends."

"Now I understand the comments you made about your big pot," he said. "You had every right to be upset, or at least not at your best. But you didn't try to cover up your tears. You just apologized for any difficulty it might have caused. That intrigued me. I like people who take responsibility for their actions and choose their own course in life—authentic people. I attempt to be that type of person, myself."

"I noticed. You handled things well, too," she said. "Nothing seems to phase you."

"Why, thank you," he said, with a smile.

"If the studio reopens soon, I expect most of us can pick up work where we left off, though sadly without Matthew's inspiration. I'm thankful we got a week of his knowledge and can't wait to get back to the wheel and see what I remember. Maybe I'll create a pot bigger than my urn."

"That's a glass-half-full response to having your special workshop cut short," he said.

"Matthew was like the father I always wanted. That seems strange to say since I only knew him for a week, but it's true. He understood how the art I've studied and my creative impulses come together in my work. We communicated like we'd known each other for years. It seems unreal that he's gone." Her voice drifted off.

Anders took another bite before continuing the conversation. "So you go back to work on Monday— design for the wine industry, right?"

"I design wine labels, slogans, and logos online for Washington wineries, half time. But work pours in at certain times of year and then dribbles off to nothing later. My employer keeps me on year round, which is great for a dependable income, but I often get stuck doing prosaic fill-in work during the low season."

"So that's why you want to throw larger pots."

"Right. If I worked for myself, as a consultant, my ceramics could take up the slack off-season. Only a minority of potters ever learns to throw the big pots. I'd have less competition than I do at present and a greater demand for my products. If I made enough money to live on, I'd have created a lovely blend of vocations."

"You've thought this through, haven't you?"

"Yes. Now I just have to quit thinking and do it." She grinned.

"That's always the hard part, isn't it?" He chuckled.

"I thought of a question after your call last night," she said. "How do you autopsy cremains? If it's gruesome, I may not want to know."

"No, not grisly at all. I was curious, too." He described the process and spent a few minutes catching her up on the investigation: the fingerprint and fiber analyses, the autopsy results, identification of the wedding ring, and the failure of the first DNA analysis on the cremains.

He mentioned that Alice had come into town with her husband's medical and dental records, too. But he held back his concerns about Quent and didn't mention Tim knowing of Matthew's life insurance policy.

"What do you do in your spare time, Anders?" Marca asked over their dessert of flan in caramel sauce.

"I co-coach a Little League team with Roy Tenison, a coworker. I'd do more, but that's the most my work schedule will allow for now. We can't always make the games, with all the schedule changes, but we divide up the weekend responsibilities and cover for each other when we have to work."

"Nice setup."

"Yes, it is. As a kid, Little League was my favorite activity, season after season. Now I impact kids in a positive way by equating sports with exercise. I love the game, the kids and the fitness."

"Sounds like fun."

"Always. A few parents are difficult, but the kids are great. Win or lose, they learn something valuable: teamwork, sportsmanship—" He turned his palms upward and smiled to complete his sentence.

"I bet having policemen who coach keeps things civil, too."

He laughed at that. "Sometimes, perhaps. At other times, well, I'm not sure anyone could make a difference."

She laughed with him.

"Roy says that once the kids realize I'm a softie, they take advantage of me. I suppose a few do. But what I usually see is that some gravitate to his tough, drill sergeant approach, while others need the arm around their shoulders, the gentle word of encouragement—my contribution to the mix."

"I bet you serve more kids by having two types of coaching."

"I hope so." He smiled. "Let's see. In addition to Little League, I've really gotten into running this past year—my unstructured thinking time. Parts of an investigation often fall together for me while I exercise.

"But also, there's a freedom to a long run that I love. In fact, I recently ran my first marathon down in Seattle, and came in around the middle of the pack. It felt great just to finish. I hope to do another one later in the year."

"A marathon. Wow. That's an impressive achievement," Marca said. "I don't do any structured exercise. But I stay in shape helping in the studio. Fifty-pound boxes of clay are as good as weights. For the rest, I dance like I breathe, and pick up new steps all the time. I also hike with my camera when the weather's dry."

"I'll keep that in mind. Maybe we can go together sometime, once the case is wrapped up, of course."

"Let's," she said. His suggestion put a grin on her face.

He likes me. Sweet!

Chapter 8

The next morning, before the potluck, Marca stopped by the P.D. to pick up Matthew's handouts for the potters. Alice had given them to Anders, but he had neglected to bring them to Marca the night before, and had called her later with an apology. He told her he'd leave them for her at the front desk.

When she arrived and collected the materials, Anders was just heading out into the parking lot.

"Marca. You caught me on the way out to canvass the neighborhood around the ceramics studio again. It's great to see you."

She walked with him to his car. Excited to catch him unexpectedly, she chatted longer than she meant to.

As she hurried back to her Civic, she saw an attractive middle-aged woman in a silver Prius back out of a parking space not far from her own. Where the Prius had parked, Marca noticed a cellphone on the asphalt. She darted over, scooped it up and waved her hands, one holding the phone, as she called out, trying to flag down the driver. The woman never glanced in her rear-view mirror but turned left out of the lot and vanished down the street.

Marca flipped the cell over in her hands looking for identification. The exterior was unmarked.

Short on time, she glanced around guiltily, saw nobody watching, and slipped the phone into her pocket. She figured she could bring it back to the P.D. after the party. She had cut her time so close already that a trip back into the building might allow her friends to arrive before she got home.

* * *

Stepping out from behind a maple tree, the tall, dark-haired man watched Marca drive away. His lips pressed together hard and his nostrils flared.

He darted to his own car and pulled out of the lot just in time to see her turn a corner ahead of him. He drove faster, just keeping her in sight. *I have to stop her. She mustn't mess with that phone.*

But when he arrived at her home, people were already climbing out of two different parked cars to hug her and go inside with her.

Just my luck.

* * *

Being a potluck, the gathering was a success from its inception. Introverts were over-represented among the ceramicists, but most had worked together for years now and looked forward to seeing each other. They were as hungry to discuss the week's events as to share the repast.

The abrupt termination of the workshop was difficult for everyone, and the loss of Matthew was exceptionally sad. Tim's bereavement was the greatest sorrow for all of them, and they offered their presence to comfort him.

Marca's home was small and cozy, and she had lit candles about the living room to accent its intimacy. In an open style, the kitchen fronted onto the main room, with an accordion panel in place of a wall. With the panel pushed back, more people could sit together. Several of those attending brought extra folding chairs, and she set them up in a rough circle that overflowed into the kitchen. Her colorful pottery decorated many of the surfaces, and the other potters milled around as if in a gallery, complimenting Marca until she felt the blood rise in her cheeks.

The food was mostly homemade or purchased from high quality delis. Only their oldest member, Mary Jane, age 93 with no kitchen or car of her own, brought supermarket fare. Her contribution was always appreciated, but especially today. She offered what none of the others could—hope for a long, active and creative life—even in the shadow of Matthew's death.

Today, the fare was particularly fine: Korean sushi, curried chicken over basmati rice, quinoa salad with pine nuts and vegetables, *dolmades*, creampuffs sprinkled with powdered sugar, croissants—both savory and sweet—made from scratch, and some of the most luscious brownies on earth. The feast was spread like treasure along the kitchen counter. Fresh squeezed lemonade in an icy pitcher capped off the offerings.

Just the scents made Marca salivate. She piled her first plate high and found a chair in the circle of friends.

"I stopped by the police department this morning to pick up materials from Alice Fyre," Marca said. "Matthew prepared them for our second week. I'm hoping that Tim can use them with us. Looks like we missed a great workshop."

"I look forward to seeing them," Tim said, wiping his mouth with a napkin.

"While I was there, I found a cellphone in the parking lot. I need to drive back over to the P.D. and turn it in right after the potluck. I was running so late, I was afraid you'd all beat me here if I stopped to do it then. I hope whoever lost it hasn't missed it yet. I know I'd go crazy without mine."

"Does anyone know when the studio will reopen?" Quent asked the group between mouthfuls.

"I asked the detective yesterday. He said that most of the crime scene work was finished. We might be able to reopen as early as tomorrow—Saturday. I think I'll give him a call when I finish my lunch and see if that still holds," Tim said.

"That means less than a week that our projects sit in plastic before we get back to them," Briana said, a hand-builder able to copy, freehand, geometric designs from a variety of cultures onto her pieces. "Excellent. The clay should still be pliable."

"Spray and rewrap them if they've dried too much," Tim said. "I bet we can finish most, if not all of them."

"Are we safe at the studio?" Kiku, the younger Korean potter asked. "I keep imagining the murderer spying on us while we work."

"I suggest that nobody stay in the building alone, especially if that back door is open," Tim said. "That's a good precaution at the best of times but especially important considering the murder."

"What did the police discover?" Lisa asked.

"Blood on the patio outside the back door of the studio with skin cells and hair in it. Broken fingernails at the back door, and a small bit of hair caught in a hinge of his broken reading glasses. DNA tests matched tests on Matthew's belongings, collected from his motel room. Also, his wedding ring was in the cremains. His wife identified the inscription. It was Matthew all right."

"Oh, no," said Lisa. "I was still letting myself hope."

"I spent a lot of time with Alice yesterday," Tim said. "Matthew had a hefty life insurance policy, and she's the beneficiary. The police found that enticing—the first possibility of any motive—and of course it shifted the investigation toward Alice and me.

"But I swear, Alice would give up the money in an instant to have him back. Poor woman. Even after all these years, they were richly in love. When she talks about him, she often ends up in tears."

Tim excused himself abruptly, his eyes blinking rapidly, and stepped outside with his cell.

Marca heard exclamations of shock. She filled everybody in on the updates Anders had supplied last night.

"The detective thought I was the killer because of my mental illness," Quent said. "I didn't like that."

"We know you'd never harm anyone," said Briana.

"There is a way you can help them narrow down the search for the killer," Marca said. "Most of you had your prints and DNA cheek-swab added to the voluntary police database. But if you didn't, the investigators found lots of fingerprints and hair in the studio, and they need to figure out which samples do and don't belong to us."

Tim reentered the room as she spoke. "I'll get my prints taken on my way home from the potluck. May I turn in the cellphone to the P.D.'s lost and found for you at the same time, Marca?"

"Thanks. That'll save me a trip." She took the phone from her pocket and handed it to Tim. Then she collected the stack of Matthew's lesson plans and passed it to him. "Here are Matthew's plans, as well."

Tim glanced through the pages. "Well, I may not be the instructor he was, but I wouldn't mind trying these ideas. We can still learn from Matthew as a class."

As they finished eating, people settled here and there with clay. Four sat at Marca's kitchen table together, building pinch pots.

"I had a strange thought," said Briana. "What if Matthew faked his death so he could be run off and start a new life in a foreign country?"

"That would mean he wanted to be something other than a highly-recognized ceramicist." Lisa said. "I can't imagine him in any other career. He clearly loved the work, and he wasn't talking retirement despite his age. Maybe you watch too many crime shows, Briana."

Several people laughed.

"It would surprise me, too," Briana said. "But something unusual happened at the studio. I doubt we'll end up saying, 'Oh of course—I should have known,' once the police figure out who the murderer was."

"I wonder if the police can identify the fist print in my pot," said Marca. "It could be Matthew's—or the killer's. I'm sure that's why they took it as evidence."

"But the fight was outside, right?" Kit asked. "No other pots were damaged. It's hard to imagine a scuffle amidst all that greenware, without shards everywhere."

"Darn it. I hadn't thought of that." Marca shrugged and shook her head. "The fist mark was probably a mistake, rather than some pivotal clue. I had hoped it might be a key factor in the case. I guess I'm kidding myself as I try to compensate for the loss of my monster pot." She laughed at her assumed self-importance.

"With all these creative minds together, we may think of some possibilities to help the police investigation," Ju-Mie, the older Korean woman said. "Anyone else have a theory about what happened?"

"I keep wondering if somebody else got pushed inside that kiln, and Matthew will still turn up. But yuck. Whoever died in there, what an awful way to go—getting burned to death," said Briana. She shuddered.

"Then where is he now? His wife says she has no idea. Seems to me like Matthew's an unlikely candidate for a kidnapping," Dave said. "What would anyone want with a ceramicist? It's not like he was some rich CEO or a dangerous spy."

"Maybe he was abducted by aliens," Lisa said, with a smile.

"We all die eventually. It's the natural cycle of nature. Yet, we really don't want to believe he's dead, do we?" Ju-Mie said.

"I certainly don't. His death is a terrible loss for me, but even more so, to the world. He was a master," said Tim. "Yet it is the most logical explanation of why he went missing. And it fits the evidence so far. I hate the thought that he lost his life because I invited him to Woodsdale." His voice dropped in volume as he spoke.

Kit, sitting next to him, leaned over and hugged his shoulders.

"Tim, did you find out if we can go back into the studio tomorrow and throw?" Quent asked.

"I confirmed it. We can," Tim said. "However, we need to park on the street and not enter the parking lot, the patio, or the kiln area yet. Our firing has to wait a little longer. But at least we can gather again in the studio and work on our pieces together."

* * *

That night, Marca called Anders and shared the homicide theories that the pottery group came up with during the potluck, as unlikely as most of them sounded.

"Did you figure out who the owner was of the cellphone I found in your parking lot?" she asked.

"Cellphone—I didn't hear about it."

"Yes. Tim said he'd turn it in at the front desk when he came by this afternoon. I thought they'd pass it on to you."

"I bet they tossed it into the lost and found cupboard. You wouldn't believe how much stuff gets turned in every day from all over the city. Most of it is never claimed. But if it was found in our parking lot, there's a fair chance we can identify the owner. What type was it? I'll look later when I get back to the office."

"I don't recall the brand, but the case color was hot pink. I'm almost certain I saw the woman who dropped it, too, but it was no one I knew. I tried to get her attention as she drove away from the spot where I found it, but no such luck. Let me know what you discover. In this curious mind of mine, little things like that tug at me."

* * *

Anders often worked through the weekend after taking on a homicide investigation, but at this point, with Quent trying to get into the studio as their only new lead, he felt he could juggle his hours around. The work he had planned for the morning was routine, mostly computer and paperwork, though important to finish.

He planned to come in early and stay late at work on Saturday so that he could take off midday Sunday for a few hours to be with the little leaguers, before returning to work. Roy Tenison usually covered the Saturday games. Anders figured that, at least this weekend, their arrangement would work out. Next weekend was still a question mark. *Who knows where we'll be in the investigation by then.* But Roy had a fairly regular schedule working traffic control. Between the two of them, Anders hoped not to need to cancel any games.

That evening, as he left for home, he checked the lost and found for the cellphone. There were eleven phones there, turned in since they last cleared out the closet. Only one matched the description Marca had given him. He pushed it into his pocket as he went out to his car.

When he got home, he changed his clothes, and then rushed back out to a coaches meeting. He left the cellphone atop his chest of drawers.

He didn't think of it again that night.

Chapter 9

The first thing Anders heard as he checked his voicemail early the next morning was Ana Nguyen's voice.

"I'm afraid I am the bearer of bad news this morning, baby. The DNA in the bone samples we tested was destroyed by heat. Sorry. I really hoped we'd ID it.

"However, what I discovered when comparing the metal in the cremains to Matthew's dental and medical records is, well, unexpected. The anomalies will interest you. In fact—uh—I'll just say that you *won't* want to miss this magic show. Give me a call."

Anders looked at the clock—6:00 a.m. He doubted she had arrived yet, but he called anyway. Her voicemail picked up, and he left a return message. "Tag. You're it, kitten."

He spent the next hour entering his interview notes from Friday's canvassing into the computer. This second round of visits still uncovered no one who saw or heard a disturbance at the pottery studio or nearby. He retained all the comments electronically, in case a person's story changed or new evidence showed up at a later time. At this point, the statements looked consistent. He frowned. *Lots more shoe leather than glory in police investigation. Not like on television.*

He poured a cup of coffee in the staffroom down the hall and greeted some co-workers as they arrived. Then he returned to his office and started through his in-box. Then, he had reports he'd fill out. *Paper work. Bleh.*

He'd learned a long time ago that if he always started from the top, reports could get buried. *In on the top, out from the bottom.* He took out a 9x14 yellow ruled notepad from his center drawer, covered the top of the in-box with it, and then turned the whole batch upside down. He lifted the box away after a few gentle taps and started to skim through the pile of data.

Lab reports. Some he had seen, but some were new. He perused them all, letting a picture of the crime take form behind his eyes.

The hair and fiber lab matched DNA from hairs to several people's latent prints. Setting aside the potters' data, he glanced through the remaining possible suspects. He'd already questioned them all. Each either had a good reason to be in the studio, was alibied for the day of the murder, or both. There was no information on the few prints still unidentified.

There were also no matches to the criminal or voluntary DNA databases except to the potters. *Nothing new here.*

He turned over the Hair and Fiber Report and scanned it. Assorted fibers, or strands of hair, might confirm the suspect's presence on the premises once caught. *But they won't help my search.*

No fiber signatures indicated traceable exclusivity. But then, who wore expensive originals to work with clay? He snorted at the image that came to mind—the potters as celebs stepping straight from the red carpet to the wheel. *Nope. Not a chance.*

University fingerprint records on Matthew were next. They matched prints found around the lab, on the door to the kiln, its controls, and in his local motel room, all as expected.

Most curious was a set of four fingerprints from his right hand, little finger at the top, where Matthew had grasped the molding around the lab's back door from the inside. Torn pieces of his fingernails were found there, too. Anders imagined Matthew standing with his back to the door when somebody grabbed him and dragged him from the studio. *Possible.*

He flipped up the next report. A sprayed latex cast of the fist print in Marca's urn backed up the theory of a right-handed victim with his back to the door. Heel skids along the floor from the black soles of athletic shoes went right past the pot. *Matthew's? Probable.*

His brain needed some down time, but he didn't want to leave for a run while waiting for Ana to come in. He put down the reports and grabbed a stack of discarded paper from the front folder of his file drawer. He leaned back in his chair, crumpled a page into a wad, and arced it towards a mini-basketball hoop centered over the blue recycle basket in the corner of his office. He shot again. And again. Each time a ball of paper passed through the hoop and into recycle, he threw his hands up into the air. Then he made a soft whistling sound that mimicked the canned cry of a cheering crowd from a computer game he used to play.

While he distracted himself, he let his intuition piece together the scene as it must have been on the day of the killing, starting with Matthew being dragged from the studio. Outside, the evidence indicated a struggle that probably ended when Matthew hit his head on the concrete patio. But how did Matthew's hefty body get from the patio to the kiln? *On the cart?* Considering the clarity of Matthew's fingerprints on the cart handle and the lack of trace evidence on the bed of the cart, that seemed unlikely. The scene slowed down and then stuck in his head. *I'm missing some vital clue at this point.*

Anders stopped the basketball practice abruptly and jotted a note. "Two suspects, working together to carry Matthew?"

Anders's phone rang. It was Ana Nguyen.

"Glad I caught you in, big boy. Move your lazy bones downstairs to my office. It's show time," she said.

* * *

Anders locked his office and was downstairs with Ana when Alice showed up at the police station. At first Alice asked for him, but when she heard that he was away from his office, she asked for the receptionist's help.

"When I was here yesterday, I must have dropped my cellphone somewhere. Did anyone turn it in?"

"Where were you at the time? In the detective's office?"

"No, I received a call after that, walking down the hall. Then I thought I dropped it into my purse just before I left the building. But I haven't seen it since."

"If it was turned in, it will be in our lost and found. Can you describe it for me?"

She told him what to look for, and he left for a few minutes. She leaned one hip heavily against the counter and closed her eyes while she waited, taking shallow, quick breaths. *Please find it.*

When he returned she couldn't help leaning forward toward him.

"Sorry," he said, "but no cellphones fit the description. Check back next time you're in the area, though. Often things get turned in later."

"Please check again, would you? There's an urgent message on it that I need to deal with right away. I didn't record the number anywhere else." Her voice, in her own ears, sounded wheedling. She tried not to let him see her wince at the sound.

"Of course," he said.

The receptionist was gone longer the second time. Alice twisted her wedding ring and picked at her cuticles as she waited, causing one to bleed. She put it into her mouth and licked away the metallic sweetness. *Please, please, please.*

But he returned empty handed, his brows clenched. "I sorted through the entire lost and found closet. I'm positive that if your cellphone were inside, I'd have found it. I'm very sorry, Ma'am."

Alice, on the verge of tears, thanked him brusquely and stumbled out with her hand over her mouth.

* * *

"You've piqued my curiosity, sweetheart," Anders said.

"Just as I planned. I've devised quite a production for you, blue eyes."

Ana wore a form-fitted suit in beige linen that accented her curves with matching heels that showcased her legs. She winked at him and posed. Then with the grand gesture of a magician, she snapped a film under two clips at the top edge of a light box.

"I call Act I 'The Mystery of the Plate.' Here's an x-ray of the repair done on Matthew's broken tibia six years ago. It's from his medical files. You can see the screws and the plate they held in place." She picked up a pen and pointed to dark places on the film.

"Okay. Looks like six screws, if I count right."

She nodded agreement. "They are consistent with the six found in the cremains. The plate should have been with them. But no go.

"These days, many mortuaries remove large pieces of metal, and most remove all metal before releasing the cremains. But if cremation occurred in the kiln, the plate should have remained with the screws.

"Now. The kiln remained unopened until a potter unlatched it on Monday morning," she said. "So nobody could have removed that plate from Matthew's remains, am I right?"

"That's what I was told, though I didn't specifically ask about the plate. I can double check."

She gave a nod. "I figured, if it wasn't removed after the firing, the plate must have been removed from Matthew's leg in a second surgery. Follow-up operations are fairly common, especially if the patient finds the hardware uncomfortable, though the screws and plate are removed in the same procedure. So I read every word of Matthew's medical records. Nothing indicates that the plate was ever removed from his leg, much less that it was removed and the screws replaced afterward."

"That fits with what Alice said. She told me about the screws and the plate, but specified that they had not bothered Matthew enough that he wanted them removed."

"We've come full circle with no solution," she said. So let's move on to Act II: 'A Trail of Dental Irregularities.'

"Check out Matthew's dental x-rays." She switched films. "Note the amalgam-filled teeth. Amalgam is rarely used for fillings these days, because it contains mercury. In fact, lots of people have had their old fillings replaced. Since Matthew's fillings were amalgam, they probably came from childhood—ancient history.

"These four films show his most recent left and right side views, taken from the inside and outside, while the remaining two films show the front teeth. All surfaces of the teeth are shown in at least one x-ray. The fillings are easy to count, all on the sides in back teeth." She pointed again with her pen. "One, two, three, four, five fillings. Clear."

"Agreed."

"I checked his previous set of x-rays to be sure I hadn't missed any, and they looked the same. No recent visits were for additional fillings."

"Okay."

"Now check the report on the cremains." With a flourish, she handed him a sheet of paper, which he skimmed.

"Eight fillings? Three more than Matthew had. Could some have broken in pieces and been counted as whole fillings?"

"I checked each one carefully for broken surfaces, under magnification, but they were whole. There were eight distinct fillings. Interesting, don't you think?"

He gave her a slow smile. "That proves that, unless somebody purposely added fillings to the mix, these were not Matthew's remains," he said.

"You're a quick one, babe. Someone else may have died in that kiln. Here's Act III: 'The Case of Incongruous Cremains.'

"You see, Mortuaries grind bone fragments, like those found in the kiln, following cremation. That way, cremated remains, which are lumpier than actual ashes, appear of even consistency throughout. Theoretically, grinding makes the families feel more comfortable examining cremains, or handling them if they decide to scatter—a popular alternative to interment.

"When I observed the number of bone fragments of uneven sizes in the sample, I assumed cremation occurred in the kiln—not in a crematorium where grinding would eliminate them. Also, the remaining metal pieces pointed to that theory.

"DNA analyses of cremains yield helpful information less than half the time to begin with. A corpse cremated twice, the second time in the extended firing cycle of a kiln, would not retain enough DNA cohesion for analysis. During the autopsy, the M.E. stated that the bone fragments fell apart with only slight pressure from the forceps. That's consistent with the studio firing being the second time these remains were burned.

"Of course, there are few instances of cremation via pottery kiln, so there are unknowns here. Perhaps anyone cremated to Cone 02 would have no DNA left, even after a single firing. I can't be certain. But why did we find bone fragments and metal if cremation occurred in a crematorium?"

"A good question," he said.

"Here's one possibility. If this person died several decades ago, their cremains would have contained bone fragments and metal as a matter of course. This corpse's immolation may pre-date the grinding of bone fragments following cremation. If the screws held a plate, it could have been removed from the cremains at that time. Or the screws may have been used without a plate."

"Your logic is perfect. I'll never be able to repay you, sweet thing," he said.

"You better believe it, hon. Good luck on the case." She reached over and squeezed his hand with the affection of a dear friend.

* * *

He phoned his captain with the news. "The cremated remains were not Matthew's, and may have come from a mortuary some years back. If you can assign me another officer to make the calls, we'll know right away."

"Not bad work, Anders, for a rookie," he heard the captain say. "But I already released more officers from regular duties than most detectives need for an investigation. Our department budget can't bring in any other subs. Important work besides yours goes on in this city. Work smarter. Figure out how to use the personnel you have."

After he hung up Anders gave a deep sigh and then stretched. He chewed his cheek for a moment, considering, and then reassigned Peter to mortuary calls. He also asked the officer to compile a list of missing persons in the area who might have been cremated in the kiln, and if possible, to locate their medical and dental records.

Until Matthew's body turned up, he must assume an abductor held him captive. If alive, the likelihood of his death increased with every hour that passed. Hostages became millstones soon after abduction, restricting the movements of their captors. Kidnappers didn't deal with them for long. *So who kidnapped Matthew? Tim, for the insurance money? Quent for some obscure reason? A stranger?*

The receptionist from the main desk cleared his throat from the doorway. "Sorry detective, but I thought you had left the building. A woman came by and initially asked for you, but didn't leave her name. She had lost her hot pink cellphone on our property. I checked, but it wasn't in our lost and found. She appeared quite upset—asked me to look again—then left. Personally, I wasn't sure she should be driving."

"Thank you. If she comes by again, please ask her name for me, will you?"

"Yep. It's on my list." The receptionist turned away.

Anders had remembered the cellphone as he dressed that morning, and brought it into the office with him. Now he took it from his center drawer and turned it over several times in his hands. The case appeared unmarked, so he removed the case and looked at the phone itself. He found no indication of who owned it.

He turned it on and called up recent messages. The bars showed a strong signal. No password protected its contents. He opened the first saved message and listened.

"Hey dearie, it's Leslie. Give a call when you're free. Nothing big here, just wanted to see how you're holding up."

He moved on to the next message. It was a sales call. He listened to two more messages without receiving any hint about the identity of the owner. The time stamp indicated that the fifth message must have come in just after Alice left his office yesterday. An electronically altered voice spoke in an inhuman tone that made the hairs on his body stand up.

"Mrs. Fyre. I have information regarding your husband's death. Contact no one about this call, especially the police. I'll call you again on Saturday at 10:00 am. Be waiting so we may talk in person. If you cooperate fully, I will offer you the thing you want most in the world. Think about it."

The caller disconnected.

Chapter 10

Anders sat for a moment and stared at the cellphone. His mind seemed to have frozen. He glanced at the clock. It was 9:45. In fifteen minutes, Matthew's captor would call Alice again. But she wasn't here to answer the call.

He burst into a flurry of action.

First he called Alice and told her he had her phone. Her voice sounded breathless as she told him she was on her way over to pick it up. She didn't mention her upcoming call. He didn't take the time to bring it up. He doubted she could arrive in time for it.

He asked the technology department for a specialist to set up a phone trace over the next few minutes.

Then Anders pondered the women in the P.D., comparing memories of their voices to Alice's. Someone needed to play her part and keep the caller on the line during the attempted trace. Officer Jessica St. Marie's voice was of a similar timbre, though their vocal patterns differed. But her office, two doors away, meant he could get her cooperation quickly. She promised to come straight over.

A bustle of preparation surrounded the two of them. Then, at 9:58, Anders and Jessica went silent. The seconds on the wall clock, which sped by so quickly just moments before, now moved about as quickly as trees grow.

The stand-in Alice inhaled and released a deep breath, shaking out her shoulders and blinking her eyes several times. She nodded once, which Anders took to mean that she was internally prepared.

"Trace ready," the tech said. "Keep him connected as long as possible." Jessica nodded. Then he left the room to monitor equipment downstairs. He left the door ajar in case he needed to reenter quietly.

It was 9:59. They waited. The clock's second hand was mired in molasses.

At 10:00 exactly, the phone played the opening phrase from a Bach fugue. Anders nodded at the woman officer, who answered the cellphone.

"Hello?" She set the phone on speaker.

The altered voice said, "Mrs. Fyre?"

"Yes. Who are you? How did you get my number? And what do you know about Matthew's murder?"

"I see you received my earlier message. Excellent. Now stop the demands and listen. Only I get to ask questions from here on out. Are you alone?"

"Yes."

"Did you tell anyone about my previous call?"

"No."

"Good girl. Will you cooperate with me?"

The officer looked at Anders.

He touched all ten fingertips together and then pulled his hands slowly apart. *Stretch out the call.*

"I—I don't know why I should. I don't know you. What information do you have, and why should I trust you?" she asked.

"Nuh-uh-uhhh. I ask the questions, remember? You are not cooperating when you ask questions."

"I remember. But in your message, you said you had information about my husband. I want to hear it."

"I know where he is."

"Where his body is?"

"That's a question. One more and I'll end this call. Believe me—I can make you wish you never heard my voice."

"Sorry. No more questions. I'll listen."

"You see, I need to trust you. If you can't control your behavior over the phone, where the pressure is minimal, I won't do business with you in real life. You must assure me that I take no risk in dealing with you."

"You can trust me. I'm not out of control; I questioned you because I'm upset and suspicious. You contacted me with information, but I don't know you. This could be some cruel ruse because I am in a vulnerable place. I just lost my husband."

"Well, I've found him. You can have him back in exchange for the two million dollars cash from his life insurance settlement."

"I thought that took seven years to release in a missing person's case."

"Not if his remains were cremated in a kiln. The coroner needs to decide about them soon. I set up the scene at the studio to help us both along, because I'm a thoughtful person. Do whatever you can to make sure the declaration occurs as expected. Once the insurance company receives your husband's death certificate, they'll pay you the money. Then you pass it on to me, and I return your husband. Easy."

"His body means little to me."

"Didn't I offer you the thing you want most in the world?"

"He's alive," she said in a whisper.

"I plan to keep him that way as long as the case moves forward without a hitch. But I won't wait forever. Neither of us wants a situation where his actual body needs to be found before the money is released. Am I correct?"

"Yes. Oh yes." Her voice cracked.

"Then you know your role. Goodbye, Mrs. Fyre."

Before she could speak again, the phone went dead.

Anders heard someone retch in the hallway. He jumped up and rushed out the office door, where he was nearly splashed with vomit. The real Alice Fyre, bent over at the waist with her hands on her stomach, puked into a planter where a rubber tree grew.

* * *

Jessica accompanied Alice to the lavatory to clean up. When they returned, Anders had brought her both a cup of coffee and one of water. He pulled up a chair for her beside his desk and she sat in it, trembling.

"I wasn't sure what you'd want." He gestured to the cups. "Hearing that call was difficult, I know. Take it easy for a few minutes, Alice, okay?"

"All right," she said, taking a miniscule taste of the water.

"Detective?" The technician spoke from the doorway. "We were successful—"

Anders interrupted him, handing him the cellphone and its pink case. "Another favor? Check this, and sweep my office. Us as well." He gestured to himself, Jessica, and Alice. "Let's be certain of our privacy."

"No problem," the tech said. "I'll be right back."

"Meanwhile, relax and rest." He directed his gaze to Alice. "We'll talk shortly, when he finishes."

The three people in the office waited quietly. Alice sipped her water.

The tech returned with a stepladder and a scanning device, and began checking for electronic signals, and visually checking all light sockets, outlets, phones, and other items in the room. He checked the cellphone, and then waved a handheld scanner over each person. "All clean here."

"Thank you," Anders said. "I appreciate the peace of mind. Now, what did you discover about the trace?"

"It was solid—no cellphone on his end. He called from a public phone at the Woodsdale ferry dock. Shall we send someone down there?"

Anders looked at the trembling Alice whose nostrils flared at the question. Her widening eyes showed panda circles underneath. He doubted she'd slept much the night before, and she looked as volatile as sweating dynamite.

"Shall I send an officer to check it out?" he asked her. He sat back, waiting for her answer—studying her.

She shook her head, slowly at first, then faster. "No. No police. Please!" Her trembling turned to deep shudders.

He nodded and turned to the technician. "Great information. But he'll call again. We need to step carefully right now. Police visibility has to remain minimal. If we send out an officer, we might give away our participation. We wouldn't want him to retaliate and harm the victim."

The technician nodded his understanding and left the room, this time closing the door behind him.

Anders turned to Alice. "How much of that phone conversation did you overhear?"

"Enough," she said. "My husband lives, but his life is in jeopardy."

"Quite a shock to all of us, but to you most of all, I'm sure," he said.

"Especially since a policewoman pretended to be me and talked with that madman. After he told me not to inform the police!" Her voice shook.

"I didn't realize whose cellphone I held until he spoke your name in his message," Anders said. "By then, his next call was due within minutes—vital evidence in your husband's case. So I asked Officer Jessica St. Marie to play your part. It was the best plan I could devise in the brief time remaining."

"When I showed up and realized who you were talking to, at first I rejoiced, assuming that if Matthew lived, we'd soon be back together," Alice said. "Then I realized he was far more likely to be dead than alive by the time I reached him, especially with this officer talking to him." She jabbed her finger at Jessica. "And I began to experience losing him all over again." She gave a whimper, then swallowed it. She set her face. Her hands made fists.

"That's harsh," said Anders. "But we can't change it now."

"When he calls again, will Officer St. Marie continue to play me? This is a terrifying game we play, me trying to sound like her playing me. I don't like it one bit." He heard a cutting edge in her voice.

"I can, yes," Jessica said. "I'd be glad to."

"But eventually I need to meet him in person with the ransom," Alice said. "What happens when he hears my real voice? He'll discover that I lied, and worse, that I'm in league with the police. That will mean the end of Matthew."

"Not necessarily," Anders said.

"You can't believe the suspect will think my voice is the same as yours," she said to Jessica. "I pray to God he never compares them."

"Same here," said Jessica. "But he's heard mine already. So all we can do is minimize the risk for the future. I'll keep your phone, and help you learn how I speak so we'll sound more alike," Jessica said. "We have the conversation taped—as a beginning. And we have until ransom day to practice together. We can do this. Voices always sound different live than over the phone."

"I store all my personal contacts in my phone, so you may not keep it," Alice stated flatly. "It's my only tie to friends back in Spokane, my lawyer, and professional contacts. I must have it back." She stood and loomed over Jessica with her hand stuck out, palm up. "Now." She appeared accustomed to being obeyed.

"I'm sorry, but the phone is evidence. It stays here," Jessica said in a calm voice. "But call me any time, and I can look up contact information you need, or play back a message. You'll have access to everything you need."

Alice gave a shriek and beat her fist against the wall. "My husband is the victim here. I am not a criminal! Why are you taking my freedom from me? You treat us like we're to blame for Matthew's kidnapping!!"

"You aren't," Anders said. "But you have no idea how often ransom situations fail to bring back the kidnapped person. We've developed best practices from multiple sources, and we follow them so that our chances of success increase. We know that people can get hurt if we trust a criminal to do what he says."

"This is intolerable. It's not going to work," Alice said. "If you had left my phone alone, this operation would be far less risky. So why should I trust you now?

"I want to talk to your superior about this. I'm going to talk to my lawyer as well. You may not jerk me around like a dog on a leash. I am an intelligent woman with little reason to cooperate with your bureaucratic B.S. And don't forget—I'm your number one specialist on Matthew."

"You are welcome to call an attorney. And I'll make the call to the chief for you, if that's what you want. Give the word at any time. But remember, I'm on your side," Anders said. "I want Matthew back safely as my first priority exactly like you do. And I can reduce the chance of him being harmed."

She sat back in her seat. "You see," Alice said in an intense but quieter voice, leaning forward toward Anders and making circumscribed gestures with her hands as she spoke, "I planned not to involve you. I understand that seeking help from the police is the 'right' thing to do. But for the first time in my life, being the good little woman doesn't interest me. Not when my husband's life is on the line. Everything changed for me once I found out Matthew was kidnapped.

"This ransom is a private transaction that concerns nobody but my husband and me. I've thought about this—the price is fair. Well worth Matthew's safety. I will follow through as he asked. So keep the police out of it!"

"I believe we can capture him at the hand-off," Anders said. "We've had success in similar situations."

"I won't take the risk. The insurance money is merely paper. I'd trade it without regret to hold my husband one more time."

"But if your husband is alive, no benefit will be paid," Anders said. "There's no perfect solution to this mess."

"Then I will take the money from our retirement savings," Alice said, her voice pressured. "Most of it is tied up in mutual funds, but they release in a day or so. That way, you don't have to worry about me breaking the law by cheating the insurance company." She sneered the last phrase. Then she sat up tall and gave orders like a military general, gesticulating as she spoke.

"We'll do this my way, detective! You won't be involved at all. It'll be my personal affair—giving away my money as I choose. I will not let you spoil my one chance to get Matthew back."

"I'm sorry, but we need to move forward, not back. I can't pretend I never heard that conversation with the suspect. It is important evidence, and I happen to have a dead person to identify and a criminal to catch."

"I don't care about your crappy pile of cremains. They can't be any deader than they are now. And as far as I'm concerned, the creep can go free. This is about only one thing for me. Bringing Matthew home alive."

"Alice, you seem to forget that we are professionals with special skills. We have experience in ransom situations and a database on the success of multiple actions taken by other departments. We'll research it before we choose what's most likely to succeed in Matthew's case. Our involvement will improve your chances of recovering Matthew alive. I'm sure of it," Anders said.

"You have how many employees in the police department?" She spat a dismissive sound. "Too many mouths gabbing. He overhears one wrong word, he discovers that the police are involved, and he kills Matthew. How many times do I have to say this! I won't have it!" Her voice snarled.

"Alice, that's unlikely—," Anders began.

But Alice jumped up, eyes bulging, covered the distance between them in one long stride and yelled in his face. "Quit Alicing me and listen!" Then she raised her hand, and slapped him hard across the face.

The room froze.

Jessica rose. "Mrs. Fyre. Step away from the detective and put your hands behind your head. You are subject to arrest for assaulting a law officer. You have the right to remain silent. Anything you say can and will be used against you in a court of law. You have the right to an attorney . . ."

Chapter 11

Matthew Fyre lay motionless in a black, coffin-like cupboard, expectant. He restrained his breathing and listened to the sounds outside his box. He heard rustles, metallic clicks and a padlock's opening chink. The door to his prison flung open, and again the stab of light from one high, bare bulb blinded him.

Although he had never experienced claustrophobia in the past, he had learned all about it during this past week. He recalled the torture of war prisoners, locked in a cabinet tall enough to stand in, but too compact to sit in or recline. He reminded himself that he was lucky; his box, though of similar size, laid flat on the floor instead of erect. Lying on his back he was able to sleep. But little else.

When he had awakened in the coffin for the first time, he found himself chained: hands and feet. The kidnapper never removed his handcuffs, but the chain was just long enough to allow him to lay his arms at his sides before the cabinet door slammed shut in his face. In that single position, he slept when-

ever the temperature wasn't frigid—and shivered
through the nights when it was.

"Hands up!"

Matthew lifted his arms like flagpoles into the
air, sight still blurred from tears in his light-strafed
eyes. He squinted at his kidnapper and recognized his
perpetual stocking mask. Even during their fight,
Matthew had never gotten a clear view of the man's
facial features.

Is today the day? He prepared to snap the whip of
his arm chain—a potential weapon should his captor
approach near enough. He waited, patient as a leop-
ard, but his prey stood slightly too far from him, as
always. Today was not the day.

Another padlock snapped. His captor affixed a
cable to the center of the chain that connected his
handcuffs.

"Feet up, legs spread!"

The third snick secured the cable to the mid-
point of the chain that hobbled his feet. The cuffs
around his ankles allowed him one twelve-inch step
at a time. During his captivity, they also never were
loosened. When he stood, the cord that connected his
wrist to his ankle chain stooped him forward like an
aged man.

"Out!"

He sat up, placed his hands on the edge of the
box, pushed himself up, and climbed out. He knew
the routine and shuffled to the corner commode
where he relieved himself in view of his captor. His
only privacy was inside the coffin.

Twice each day, he estimated, his captor permit-
ted him out of his cupboard to eat in this partially finished root cellar. Musty smelling, tasting of dust, the
drab room was windowless. *After my box, it is paradise.*

His abductor said little beyond the orders he
gave. When Matthew asked questions, his captor told

him to shut up. Once, when he persisted, he was shut back into his cupboard without receiving food or water.

He changed his behavior after that, needing his strength. Now he spoke in a soft tone and asked no questions. Usually, he got nothing in return, but every couple of days the man spoke a sentence or two. None of it proved helpful so far, but Matthew stored every word in memory. It was a powerful freedom that he retained.

"Sit and eat."

He did so with a small groan. Only when he sat for a meal did his posture approach normal. His captor served him finger food—thin sandwiches mainly—on paper plates without plastic-ware that he might steal and break to form a sharp edge.

His water came in plastic bottles, lids already removed. He could throw one, full, but he doubted it would stun his jailer. Still, he held that option in mind. He dismissed no possibility outright.

"Good sandwich, thanks," Matthew said, testing whether this was a talkative day.

The man grunted in response.

Guess not.

A long drink of water half-emptied the 16-ounce container. He'd feel the need to urinate before his next release, but he swallowed every drop to lubricate his brain. He needed sharp thinking once his escape opportunity materialized. He was dehydrated already, he was certain, with an intake of one quart of water per day.

"The water's good, too. I wouldn't mind another bottle."

This comment didn't elicit a grunt—he might have just addressed an empty room.

"Back in the box."

His abductor unfastened the cord that joined the chains to his foot and handcuffs using the reverse procedure—feet then arms up while the man removed the padlocks. Matthew watched his assailant's method, counting to himself. *He takes several seconds more to unlock than to lock the padlocks—a better chance to surprise him.* He filed the information into his growing store of knowledge. *One day—.*

The box slammed shut, and he heard the outside lock snap to. His back ached to release his shoulder blades on the hard boards. It had begun to feel good. As if from a distance, he noted the workings of his mind. He both wanted to stay out of the box and to return so he could relax his unnatural posture. He resisted the positive thought about his prison. *I will not adjust to this incarceration.*

He is Enemy.

* * *

Anders cut Jessica St. Marie off using a gentle voice. He had not moved since he was struck, and the outline of Alice's palm shone scarlet on the left side of his face. He looked at the other officer who was holding her handcuffs ready.

"I have no plan to arrest a grieving woman on the edge of despair, Jessica. Unless she is likely to hit someone again."

He shifted his gaze. "Alice?"

Alice was still standing, her face white, her breathing quick, and her hands behind her head. "I'm sorry. I never hit anyone before. It's just—I have this fissure inside me and you gouge into it every time you fail to hear me. I was trying to defend myself—and my Matthew."

"I understand that now. So no more violent outbursts?"

"No."

"All right, you may lower your hands. Please take a seat. I have heard every word you said. Let me summarize your position back to you. You tell me if I missed anything, okay?" He did so.

"You didn't miss anything." Her face appeared less pallid.

"Would you do me the favor of summarizing what you heard from Jessica and me so I'm sure we're all on the same page, please?"

Alice did. Her color was better.

"Do you have anything to add," he asked Jessica.

She shook her head—a negative.

"Okay, Alice. Now. Let's continue this discussion. You said that you were afraid that your husband's abductor would hear about the operation to seize him during the handoff. In the years I've worked here, not one leak from the police has occurred. Confidentiality has never been compromised," said Anders.

"Who cares about the past? I don't believe you can possibly keep this quiet today. Please. My exchange with the kidnapper must be need-to-know. Only secrecy will save Matthew's life."

"All right. I can work from that point of view. I'll involve as few new people as possible in the case." Anders said. "And I'll swear everyone, past or present, to secrecy, even within the department."

Jessica nodded. "I can handle that too."

"During the handoff, you have to keep him from seeing any cops. Consult me on every step of your plan—and give me veto power. Remember, I'm the one who has the most to lose here—not you or anybody else! We must work this out together."

"Fair enough," said Anders. "Now, I trust the technician who swept this office earlier. If he inspects the phone in your hotel room, he can probably find a way to link us to you, whenever the call comes. So you can listen in."

"Then send him over to the hotel," Alice said. "But please, please, please be careful. For Matthew's sake."

"I'll do everything in my power to protect you both," he said. His voice left no doubt he meant what he told her.

* * *

When Marca arrived at the studio, she was surprised at the dust from fingerprinting that remained. She was also amazed that all of Matthew's tools and the pieces he had thrown as demos had been removed as possible evidence. The notebook he had left by the cart was also missing.

She took a deep breath and walked into the glaze room. Matthew's new glazes still sat in their buckets. She released the lungful of air with a laugh. *I can't wait to try them.* She walked back into the main room, and spoke to Briana.

"I'm glad Tim got Matthew's week two notebook and handouts," she said. "And his glazes. Nothing else from last week is left."

"You're right," Briana said and sighed. "It's all too awful. I wonder if this place will ever seem the same." She shook her head.

Luckily, Marca had her own notebook tucked in her locker, and she went to fetch it. All week she had taken careful notes; so she referred back to the discussion of throwing large pieces in sections.

Wedging several heavy balls of clay, she set them, with her tools, a slop bucket, and a sponge, onto the ledge of her wheel. On the wheel itself, she affixed a wide bat. She pulled up the tallest stool she could find that would still let her throw. She didn't want her bent elbow to limit the height of her piece.

Then she announced to the room, "Here goes, mudpeople. Time to create another humongous pot!"

Several soft cheers of affirmation accompanied her as she slapped a massive hunk of ruddy stoneware onto the bat, squeezed water onto it from the sponge, and leaned her shoulder into centering it for her first segment.

* * *

At the end of the afternoon, Marca lost her first three clay segments while trying to join them into one. The clay was so pliable that the structure collapsed of its own weight while she attempted to thin out the joins on the turning wheel. She stepped hard on the pedal that stopped the wheel and looked at the formless mound of wet clay in front of her. The sight made her bones ache.

Grimly, she threw three more segments, and wrapped them in plastic to harden up until she returned. She tried to recall the exact dryness of the clay when she assembled her first urn and how her hands had felt as she pulled it up tall. But she could no longer be certain how the two attempts differed. The memories swirled together in her mind like the spinning of her wheel. She cleaned up her area—a more tedious task than usual.

The potters put their work away. Marca cleaned her tools and washed her hands. Once again, her front was covered with mud, but it only made her feel dirty. She rolled a bead from clay she picked off her shirt and stared at it for a long moment before turning to leave.

"Bye, mudpeople," she said from the door.

"Look who's talking!" Kit said.

As low as she felt, Marca couldn't help but smile back.

Crossing to where she parked her car, she saw movement on the street in her peripheral vision. She stopped and leaned closer, counting eight legs. A large wolf spider walked down the middle of the road. *How did you get there, big guy?* She bent down and encouraged him onto her hand so she could remove him to safety. *I hope you—.*

She jerked erect as she heard a yell. Tires shrieked, and a black SUV swerved toward her. *No!* Adrenaline squirted into her heart and she dove to a roll, straining to reach the niche of protection between her car's front bumper and the car parked ahead of hers. A hot asphalt smell filled her nostrils and her fingernails scrabbled for purchase.

One of her knees thudded into her tire and prevented her right leg from clearing the road. She struggled to pull it to safely, but the front right tire of the SUV smashed down on her calf. Bone snapped.

She screamed at the spike of agony that lit up neurons all the way to her brain. Before her scream ended, the rear tire ran over the leg as well.

Her eyes fixed forward, Marca gasped to breathe past her pain. Instinctive survival mode prepared her body to fight whatever danger came her way in the next moment. She sensed movement where none should be at her side and swiveled her head to identify the threat.

The spider climbed off of her wrist and walked away, at an unconcerned spider-pace, down the gutter.

Chapter 12

Another potter darted to her side. "Are you okay?" Lisa asked. "I saw the car speed right for you, and I yelled." She tried to assist Marca to a sitting position, but when the injured leg moved, a shriek escaped from Marca's mouth.

"No, no! My leg."

"You can't leave your leg out in the street. The driver may come around the block and go at you again. Here, slide your left arm over my shoulder. You need to move to the curb. We'll make it quick."

"No, please!" Marca cried, but she grabbed Lisa. She threw her head back and keened as Lisa half-lifted her and dragged her back until her crushed leg lay between the two cars, away from danger.

"Here's the curb. Sit down. Okay."

Marca cried out again and tears ran down her face as she eased onto the curb. She gagged, and Lisa thought Marca might puke on her, but she curled her head down to rest on her good knee, swallowing hard several times instead.

"Lean against me and try to relax." Lisa dialed 911 on her cell and spoke into it. She kept it against her right ear even after she stopped speaking. With her left arm, she supported the panting Marca.

Marca moaned with every exhalation, and her body leaned, heavy, against Lisa's side. Lisa wasn't sure her friend was fully conscious, even though she still reacted to the pain of her crushed leg.

"I have an ambulance two minutes from your location," the 911 responder reported into Lisa's ear.

Marca caught her next breath in a sob, and opened her eyes. "Everything is spinning," she said. "Make it stop!"

"Shhh," Lisa said. "Nothing is spinning. Put your head down. Hold on to me if it will help. I'm not moving, Marca."

In the distance, Lisa heard the ambulance siren. She bit her lower lip. *Hurry. Please hurry!*

Then the ambulance was there, and two EMT's jumped out.

The male EMT knelt beside the women and checked Marca's status, shining a light into her eyes. Her face had gone greenish-white, her eyes had rolled back, and her head lolled on her neck. "Marca? Marca! Can you hear me?" the EMT said, but there was no response. He laid her onto the sidewalk on her back.

Lisa squeezed her hand.

Together, the EMT's carried over a stretcher with a balloon splint, a blanket, and a blood-pressure cuff on top. The man took Marca's blood pressure while the woman slipped the deflated splint under the upper part of Marca's leg. Then, pushing it against the ground, she slid it down into position behind the break and pressed a button to inflate it.

Marca made a weak cry, and then went quiet again. Lisa hoped that Marca remained unconscious until the leg was treated. *The pain must be unbearable.*

"Her blood pressure just dropped. Get her onto the stretcher and treat for shock," the man said. They lifted Marca onto the stretcher, elevated her legs slightly, and covered her with the blanket. This time, Marca didn't react.

"Please. Tell me how I can help," Lisa said, begging for some task to occupy her hands and mind.

"I think we have everything in hand," the man said.

"May I accompany her?"

The female EMT gave Lisa the name of the hospital, as she mounted into the ambulance on an automatic lift with Marca. She covered Marca's face with an oxygen mask and secured her, then latched closed the rear doors.

The male EMT started the motor.

When he drove away, lights flashing and siren recalling Marca's screams, Lisa ran into the studio to tell the remaining potters what had happened. Then she flew to her own car and broke the law as she sped to the hospital.

* * *

The Emergency Room receptionist took down all the information Lisa could offer, then told her to have a seat and wait. After the tumult of the past half hour, Lisa had difficulty slowing her expectations to the speed of the minute hand on the clock. Lisa forced herself to wait until an interminable hour passed, though she checked her watch every few minutes. Then she returned to the desk and asked for an update on Marca.

"Your friend was admitted, and her leg is being cared for. Did a family member come with you?"

"No."

"Do you know her insurance information?"

"I brought her purse. I found it by the car after the ambulance left. Hold on and I'll look." She hesitated for a moment, reluctant to breach the sanctity of

Marca's purse. Then she scrabbled around inside, pulled out Marca's wallet in relief, and after shuffling through a handful of cards, presented the insurance card with pressured speed.

The unflappable receptionist appeared not to notice Lisa's agitation. Her movements were deliberate. In an emergency room situation, she probably had to ignore people's uneasiness in order to function, but Lisa didn't find the method supportive right now. She watched the woman photocopy the medical card, enter data into her computer, and print a page that she stapled to the personal information form Lisa had filled out earlier.

"Okay, here's her card back. Thank you." The receptionist turned away.

"Wait. When will I find out more? May I see her?" Lisa asked. "I'm concerned about her, and I've been waiting for over an hour already.

"Let me check with the doctors. It may take awhile yet, if they are still working on her. I can't interrupt treatment—nor would I want to."

"No. Of course not." Lisa felt heat rise in her face, as if a grade-school teacher had just told her off in class. She returned to the waiting area to sit for another unyielding stint of slow-motion clock watching.

She realized that she still held the handful of cards in her hand, and tapped them into an even pile that she could slip back into the slot in Marca's wallet. She saw that the top one was Detective Johanson's business card. Before she could convince herself otherwise, she pulled out her cell, and dialed his number. She had to do something.

"Thank goodness you're still there. This is Lisa, one of the potters."

"Yes, Lisa. What's up?"

"Marca was hit by a car. I'm at the Emergency Room waiting to hear if she's okay, but it's taking for-

ever. I think her leg was broken. I didn't know whom
to call, but I had your card. I don't suppose it's really
your business but—"

"I'll be right over," he said, interrupting her.

* * *

Anders shut up his office for the day, locking
away the sensitive information. He doubted he'd
make it back in tonight.

When he arrived in the Emergency Room, he
found Lisa, still waiting.

"Will they tell you anything?" she asked. "I
think they avoid talking to me because I'm not a family member. But I'm the one who called the ambulance."

"My badge usually helps," he said. He went to
the receptionist's desk and held a short conversation
in a low voice. He returned to Lisa with a smile on his
face.

"She told me that the doctors took Marca into
surgery about an hour and a half ago, and they are
still with her in the O.R. She's unsure when the sur-
geon will finish. But if we want to wait, we can visit
Marca for a short time after she awakens from the anesthetic and is taken to her room."

"That's almost what she told me, but without
mentioning the surgery. I called my husband earlier
and told him I was at the hospital with a friend so he
won't worry. As long is it doesn't get too late, I want
to wait."

"Tell me about the accident. Did you see it happen?"

"Yes, from behind, anyway." Lisa described it in
detail. "The strange thing is, I swear that the driver of
the SUV intended to hurt Marca. The car pulled away
from the curb a block away just after she started
across the street. Then, when she paused to examine

something on the roadway, he gave it a spurt of gas, swerved, and bore down on her before she had a chance to get away. But why?"

"Hmm. She found an important bit of evidence for the investigation yesterday. My theory is that the person who attacked Matthew was making sure Marca couldn't share anything she discovered from it."

"What was it?" Lisa asked.

"I'd rather not say. The fewer people who know the details, the better—especially since we're dealing with a suspect who gets nervous enough to attack them. But when I get a chance, I'll see what Marca thinks."

"So it did turn out to be police business. Now I don't feel quite so silly about my call to you."

"Always call, please. I would have come regardless of whether it appeared work-related. Too often, people linked with a crime find themselves in danger. Only later do they realize it was related to the case. I feel partly responsible, since I didn't warn her of the possibility. I would have preferred that nobody got hurt."

Ahead of them, a woman in surgical scrubs emerged through a set of doors that opened from the inner bowels of the E.R. After a quick check with the receptionist, she called out Anders's name.

He rose and extended a hand to Lisa. "Come with me. You may not be a family member, but if anyone has a right to hear the news about Marca, it's you." She let him pull her up from her seat.

"I'm Doctor Kim," the doctor said, handing them each a business card. "We just completed operating on Marca's leg. She was lucky that the vehicle ran over her calf without hitting the knee, which was only twisted. She could have lost the leg."

"Oh my God," said Lisa.

"There are two bones in the calf. Her fibula, the smaller bone, broke in two places. The tibia, or shinbone, is unbroken, which is great news. The shinbone will serve as a natural splint—a support during healing. I expect the breaks will heal completely."

"So she'll be okay?" Lisa wanted to be certain she understood.

"I expect so, though the leg will need therapy. She's in the recovery room right now, but will be moved to room 245 in 15 or 20 minutes. You may have a brief visit with her once she's settled in."

Dr. Kim looked hard at the detective. "She'll feel groggy from the anesthetic and the meds, and may not think clearly enough to answer questions. She needs sleep more than conversation tonight."

"Thank you doctor. I am concerned about her safety here," Anders said. "We believe the hit-and-run may have been deliberate—spurred by a crime investigation. May I post an officer outside her door to check who goes in and out?"

"As long as she assents to it, yes. The nurse can give your officer the names of the medical team, who should be allowed free access. But you may ask her to review the names of visitors before the guard allows them admittance. Let her make the call."

"I'll do that. Thank you for taking care of her leg." Anders said.

"That's why we're here."

Before going up to Marca's room, Anders called his captain and requested a guard for Marca's door, and an officer to secure and protect the new crime scene. Once again, the captain was pleased with the progress, but unhappy with the number of personnel Anders was tying up in his investigation.

Next, Anders spoke to Ana about inspecting the new crime scene. Then he put away his cell, looked at Lisa and said, "Ready to go up?"

"More than ready," she said, giving him a thin smile.

* * *

Two orderlies finished repositioning Marca onto her bed as the visitors arrived. She looked like a Halloween ghoul: her eyelids nearly closed, her hair a mess, an IV in one arm, a blood pressure cuff on the other, a blood gas monitor clipped to a forefinger, and squares of gauze taped to her palms, knees and chin. She had scraped herself on the road as she attempted an escape from the oncoming SUV. Her upper lip was swollen, too, and Anders guessed that she bit it during her attempted escape.

An orderly propped Marca's leg on a pillow. Her toes bulged purple out of the open end of her left slipper. The other assistant removed the slipper and rolled a bootie-sock onto Marca's swollen foot. Anders saw Lisa's shoulders relax once the blood-engorged toes were no longer visible.

"Someone did you wrong," Lisa said. "You look like hell, mudwoman."

"Thanks for res-rescuing me," Marca's tongue sounded thick and it tripped over her words.

"No problem. Does it hurt?"

"No, but 'm so dopey, can hardly open m' eyes."

"Hope the leg heals fast. I have plans for you," Anders said.

"Welcome to m' party. Emesis basin, anyone?"

"Uh, no thanks," Anders said.

"Gotta quit mee'ing like this," Marca said.

"I agree entirely," he smiled. "Because you need to stay out of the hospital, young lady."

"I invited him here, Marca. We think that SUV hit you on purpose," Lisa said, interrupting their play.

Marca's eyes almost opened normally for a moment. "Moved fast."

"The detective believes that the driver may be the same man who accosted Matthew," Lisa said.

"He may have feared exposure," Anders said.

"Wow," Marca said.

"Did you get a look at the driver?" he asked. "Or the license plate?"

"A guy. No plate," Marca said. "Sorry, need sleep."

"One more thing," he said. "I set a guard on your door for your protection. He'll announce your visitors before admitting them so you can make sure they're friends you want to see. Okay?"

"Sure," Marca said. "'m I 'n danger?"

"Possibly. We'll discuss the details when you're more alert. Meanwhile, better safe, right?"

"Righ—." Her eyes closed involuntarily.

As they tiptoed away, Anders thanked the guard, Peter Landsbury again, and briefed him about Marca's needs.

On the way down in the elevator, Lisa spoke up. "Detective, you don't need to get the license plate number of the SUV from Marca. It branded itself into my brain as I watched the back of the vehicle speed toward Marca. I repeated it to myself about 50 times to be sure I memorized it. The car was a black Chevy, and the license number was RCV787."

Anders took out a small notebook and a pencil. "Terrific information, Lisa. This is going to help a lot. Thanks."

"Marca is a close friend. Any other way I can assist her, please be sure to let me know, okay?"

"I will. Thanks for getting help for her this afternoon." He shook her hand in one of his, and then covered it with his other hand and smiled.

* * *

Although it was late, Anders visited Marca's car, reviewed the notes of the officer on duty, and sketched and photographed the area. Starbuck's had closed, and most parked cars had departed, including the one in front of Marca's that had framed her hidey-hole.

He saw where she sat on the curb by the two light splotches of blood where her scraped hands braced the concrete for support. He set markers by the spots, and one by the tire mark in the street. Then he adjusted the crime scene tape so that one narrow lane constricted traffic passage to the far side of the road for 2 blocks. He left both sets of notes with the guard for the criminalist's review.

Anders also requested two traffic cops during peak driving times and cautionary signage from the captain, despite being reminded that the department had a shortage of personnel. The side street rarely grew busy, but Anders knew the pre- and post-work hours would challenge a single officer.

Lisa would know where the SUV had parked. He hoped it was within the area he had roped off. Once she reviewed the site with him he'd reopen the street to regular traffic. Having done all he could, he shook the hand of the guard and left.

He drove home, yawning. He thought he'd better pick up some fast food for a late dinner on the way, as it was too late to cook. *Heck, it's after midnight. They'll probably be selling breakfast burritos by now.*

* * *

During the darkest hours of the night, a tall, dark-haired man approached officer Peter Landsbury where he sat guarding Marca's door. The man smiled at Peter, looking relaxed and apologetic at the same time.

"Hey. I wondered if you'd mind if I looked in on Marca for a couple of minutes," he asked.

"Well, as you can imagine, I'm supposed to clear all visitors with her before I let them enter," the guard said.

"A great idea when there's need for security, but I imagine she's asleep right now, and I don't want to awaken her. After all she's been through, well, it would reassure me to watch her rest peacefully for a few. You know how it is."

"I sure do. Go take a quick look. As long as it's you, heck, I don't see any harm." Peter smiled.

The man slipped quietly into Marca's hospital room and stared at her as she slept. He licked his lips as if he could taste her suffering. Sorry he hadn't eliminated her, he also felt relief that her injury was not severe enough to kick up the investigation another notch. He wanted to prolong his game.

Clearly, she wouldn't go home tonight. He breathed in a rush of power as he leaned over her motionless form. He could do anything to her. His smile turned to a leer. *I could snuff her out before anyone could stop me. They have no idea who they are dealing with.*

He remembered the officer standing guard outside the door and knew he needed to leave before he brought more attention to himself. But he enjoyed seeing her helpless like this. So he paused for another long moment while he imagined how easily his fingers would fit around her neck.

Chapter 13

Anders phoned Ana in the morning. "Any news, my beauty?"

"Hey, blue eyes. Nothing yet on the new crime scene, but I don't expect much. Samples of Marca's blood and some tire tracks were all I found."

"I suppose you're right."

"But only a few sets of prints remain to ID from the original crime scene. We're making progress."

"If the suspect in Matthew's abduction is the one who hit Marca, we're looking for a male," Anders said.

"Murderers and kidnappers usually are, but I appreciate knowing for sure. Anything else?"

"I got the license plate of the SUV from Lisa last night. She had the presence of mind during the hit-and-run to memorize it. Talk about a loyal friend. And she didn't leave the hospital last night until I did."

"I could do with more friends like that," she said.

"A hospital visit with Marca is next on today's list. I'll let you know what I learn."

"I appreciate that. Let's nab this one, detective."

"My plan, exactly, honey bear."

* * *

Marca's hospital room was bright. White daisies sporting bright golden centers mixed with multicolored freesia and gave the room a homey feel. Yellow roses of friendship peeked through the feathers of a live miniature fern. Ivy was espaliered into the shape of a heart, and a blue balloon swayed above its planter. The potters had visited this morning, Anders saw, because the flowers were arranged in handmade pots in subtle hues.

"How do you feel today?" he asked Marca. He sat down in a chair by her bedside.

She smiled. "Like my leg got run over by an SUV, for some odd reason. Then the pain meds kick in and I doze and dream strange things. I'm not sure which is preferable. You're not a dream by chance, are you?"

"No," he laughed. "I'm very much real, strange or not. And I was here last night, too. Do you remember our visit?"

"Let me see." She paused with a thoughtful look on her face. "You were here with Lisa, right? The memory is so foggy I thought I'd imagined it. Morphine creates some amazing fantasies. You believe my injury was no accident, if I recall correctly."

"Bingo. You just won the prize." He smiled at her, and then told her what Lisa had seen. "My working theory is that the suspect figured you might become a dangerous impediment to his anonymity after you found the cellphone."

"Me? Dangerous?" She blinked several times as if not sure whether she was in a narcotic dream.

"Here's an update on the case. But please, keep it between us two."

"Okay. I like suspense."

He caught her up on the case progress, including the abductor's call to Alice's cellphone demanding Matthew's life insurance death benefit. "If he believes you heard his message, we have motive for his actions. He may have decided to give you other concerns to block the call from your mind. Or worse, he might have tried to kill you—and eliminate any threat. In that case, he'll come after you again, I'm afraid."

"I mentioned the cellphone at the potluck, and Tim offered to return it to the Police Station. I didn't talk about it anywhere else, though," Marca said.

"Maybe he saw you pocket the phone, followed you home, and eavesdropped on the conversation during the potluck. Or perhaps one of the potters knows him and mentioned the cellphone when talking to him afterward. We don't know that he's a stranger."

"That's creepy—listening at my window. Yesterday, Tim called you from my porch about the studio re-opening. I wonder if he saw the guy while he was outside?" Marca asked. "If I remember correctly, Tim made his call just after he told us the amount of the Fyre's insurance policy."

"Then the suspect may have heard that as well. I'll have to check with Tim. Thanks for the lead.

"I have an important question for you, though, so take your time before you answer. Did you get a look at the person driving the SUV that struck you? Do you remember anything about him?"

"Hmm, let me think. I half-glimpsed a man with bushy, dark hair. That's all I really remember."

Anders whisked out his cellphone. "Tim? Marca and I are at the hospital. I've got a question. When you phoned me from the potluck, did you see anybody near Marca's property?" He paused. "Will you work with a police artist? A drawing of his face would help a lot. We'd also find out whether Marca saw the same man in the SUV that hit her." Another pause. "I'll have him call you."

"What did he see?" Marca asked.

"A man walking the boundary between your neighbor's house and yours. At the time, he figured it was somebody who was supposed to be there— maybe a guy who lived next door. But it could have been the suspect leaving the spot where he had crouched beneath your side window and listened to the conversation. He probably moved away when Tim opened the front door. If Tim can help create a likeness for us, maybe you can ID him."

"I'll try, but—." She shrugged.

"Whatever you remember helps. When do you leave the hospital?"

"This afternoon or tomorrow. Depends on Dr. Kim's report when she examines me later. But I've eaten today, and I have no fever. She said that if both bones had broken, or either been crushed, I'd be a whole lot worse now—not that healing counts as entertainment." She stuck out her tongue.

"Can you stay with a friend or family for awhile? You'll need to stay off the leg anyway, and it's better if this guy doesn't know where you are."

"Yikes. I'll call some friends."

"Hopefully somebody can pack up what you need, and deliver you wherever you decide to stay. But call me if things don't work out."

"Can you get my car home for me? I can't drive for awhile, and I don't want it parked on a public street."

"Sure. No problem. Call me when you're settled in, so I know that you're safe."

She didn't realize, until he left, just how much she had enjoyed seeing him again. The room seemed darker without him in it. She closed her eyes with a sigh and let the pain meds carry her away into sleep.

* * *

Marca arranged to stay at Lisa's house. Ju-Mie and Briana offered her a room as well. It seemed to Marca that the potters felt an irrational responsibility for her injury. *As if they somehow failed to stop the car attack.*

She recalled how helpless she felt when Matthew vanished, and how emotional. After this second shock, she was relieved that she wouldn't be alone at home, especially at night. Hopefully, caring for her would help Lisa feel better, too.

After all, the house was roomy. Lisa and her husband, who traveled for work, were hoping to start a family soon. He had left just this morning on another trip, a longer one than usual. But she refused to stay until she became a burden. Just until Lisa's husband got back. *Two weeks maximum.*

* * *

"How is the leg healing?" Lisa asked when she picked Marca up.

"They provided crutches to keep weight off it as I move around. I need to elevate it when I sit or recline. And I take the pain pills for a couple of weeks yet. It's neither convenient nor comfortable, but at least I still have a leg to complain about."

"Your quick reaction probably saved your life."

"Your yell saved me." She shuddered. "I bent over to help a spider off the road, like an idiot. 'Heart on my sleeve,' my mother always said. But the street was empty when I crossed, and usually there's no traffic there. Who could have known?"

"No need to blame yourself. The kidnapper was out to get you. Don't let him twist your best intentions—make you second-guess yourself. We live in a safe city where most people go out of their way to help others. And it's a caring impulse that made you stop to help another creature.

"The only weird thing is that it was a spider," she said, and stuck out her tongue.

Despite herself, Marca laughed.

* * *

When she parked in front of Marca's apartment, Lisa helped Marca onto her crutches and into her living room.

"Thanks so much," Marca said as she clomped over to her couch and sat down.

Lisa smiled. "Tell me where to find what you need and I'll pack it for you. No need to stress your leg."

"Will you start with my computer bag? I need my laptop and some peripherals so I can work mornings."

"No problem. That's your pack?" She pointed to a teal backpack under the desk.

"Right. Thanks." While Marca had waited to be released from the hospital, she listed the items she needed for her stay at Lisa's. She passed Lisa the inventory. "This shows what else I'd like to take along, if you don't mind."

"I don't. I'm looking forward to helping you get well, mudwoman."

Limping around on crutches fatigued her and her injured leg throbbed in its cast whenever she stood upright. *How many hours since my last pain pill?* While Lisa packed, Marca elevated it, but that made it hurt as well as the blood flowed back out of it. She yearned for a nap, first thing, once she settled in at Lisa's. She was already out of cope for the day.

* * *

Anders reported to Alice that afternoon. "The Insurance Company gave us the go-ahead to send them Matthew's fake death certificate. If someone contacts them, an employee checking the records will see everything in order for the settlement.

"Our department plans to announce Matthew's death to the news agencies in the morning. Will you place an obituary in the paper today? Hopefully, that will get the suspect off of Marca's back, and speed up his next call to you."

She squared her shoulders. "I'll write the obit, but this whole deception makes my stomach hurt. This better work, Johanson. I'm depending on Jessica and you to save Matthew. Don't you dare let anything go wrong!" She wore her Chanel sunglasses like battle armor.

"It will be fine. She'll convince him that you're ready for the exchange. Then, it should go like clockwork. I have a plainclothes team that is ready to go. They'll be all around you, incognito, when he comes for the money."

"Well only use those you need, and don't tell me who they are. I don't want to know. Since I didn't call the police in on this ransom affair, I still plan to play this straight with him. I'll do my part just fine. You keep those cops out of his face. Don't you get Matthew hurt."

"I hear you. I believe that the suspect saw Marca pick up your cellphone; we assume he recognizes you as well. As our primary witness to his calls, you will be next in his sights if he kills your husband rather than releasing him. You're up to this?"

She stood tall, her face set into grim lines, her hands in fists. "I'm ready. This is what wedding vows are about—the for-better-or-worse part. Whatever happens, I'm committed to Matthew's release."

"We'll supply what personal protection we can. We can't guarantee your safety, but we'll come as close as possile."

* * *

Matthew was smart, and a survivor. As a soldier in Vietnam, he'd been taught to expect torture if he was captured. His preparation included several ghastly role-plays. He remembered how a recently released POW had spoken to his unit in a dull monotone about his experiences. The fellow's spare description created pictures in vivid color that stuck in Matthew's memory throughout his deployment, though he tried hard to forget them.

The understanding Matthew had gained in the war made this current situation more manageable. He focused on his desire to relax in his prison and engulfed it in the exceeding weariness he experienced each time the lid swung shut. *I will not think one positive thing about this coffin.*

A routine he devised helped him retain his fitness while it supported his sanity: tighten and relax each muscle group 100 times; repeat the exercise five times in succession. When he stood, released from the box, and especially if he had exercised recently, his muscles twitched readiness. His routine structured the time in darkness and kept panic at bay. He stayed active, aware of time's passage but too involved in escape-oriented tasks to overthink his situation. Mental fitness supported physical fitness.

* * *

The second-floor guestroom Lisa had set up for Marca was ivory colored, decorated with pale blue trim and a hand-painted cobalt blue design around the top, just below the ceiling. Throw pillows of the same tones, on her bed, made the room cheery. A large mirror on the wall facing the bed made the little room look larger than it was. Sunshine flowed in warm through the window at her side.

Marca squirmed, uncomfortable in Lisa's comfy house. Though her friend was hospitable, Marca rarely spent nights away from home. She didn't know how to find little things she needed, and she hated feeling helpless. The newness of everything wore on her.

Her pain added to the stress of the strange place. Finding serenity was an arduous challenge. At odd moments, she broke into tears, which fed her old fears that she would go crazy. She took a deep breath and let it out slowly. *I don't have to control everything—I need to let it go.*

She got up to use the adjoining bathroom, hoping the action would distract her overactive mind. But the tip of her crutch caught in the duvet that had fallen partway onto the floor. Trying to shake it loose, she lost her balance, and sat back on the bed heavily. She gritted her teeth while a wave of pain shook her. Then, tears in her eyes, she tried again.

When she finally sat on the toilet, she squeezed herself and rocked while her breath came faster. Dizziness made her realize she was hyperventilating and she grimly set about reestablishing her normal in- and exhalations. *Slow deep breaths. Slow down. Slow.*

Her emotions kept spiraling off into wayward patterns, something neither she nor Lisa needed. Her presence, she feared, created a negative atmosphere for Lisa. The thought wouldn't leave her mind: *She's unsafe with me here.*

She flushed and then hobbled back to her bed, exhausted by her efforts. Obsessing over fear was unacceptable. It didn't represent the positive person she had spent years training. So she struggled harder to control herself. But the tension made the pattern of unwanted thoughts start all over again.

Lisa partly understood the expectations Marca held of herself, after hearing part of her early history, but that didn't help Marca feel supported. Instead, she found herself acting crabby around her friend.

"I will take care of you, like it or not, mudwoman," Lisa had said as she helped Marca crawl into bed, and unpacked her things for her into half the closet and two empty dresser drawers. Lisa's patience seemed unending, her calm smile inalterable.

Knowing that Lisa had to work during the day gave Marca some relief from her concerns. Once Lisa left, she had one less person to protect if the attacker approached again. Yet after her friend left for the day, Marca's helplessness took over. She felt sorry for herself and couldn't wait for her friend to come home. She groaned. *I can't do anything!*

Dizziness after she took her pills, or throbbing pain as the medication waned, made her prefer lying still in bed over getting up on her crutches to get the things she needed. The trip down the stairs appeared more like an extreme survival trek.

She grabbed the three remotes and attempted to turn on the TV but fumbled them. *Just think. Lisa showed you how they work.* When she finally got the picture to come on, there was no sound. She thumped the remotes onto the bed beside her, giving a squeak of frustration.

She chafed at her confinement. *Get yourself some microwave popcorn downstairs.* But she couldn't talk herself into getting up. She denied herself that ordinary comfort in order to keep her injured leg immobile. *I'm trapped.*

She tried on a smile, hoping her mood would follow her action. That worked for her at times. But her mind kept wandering off, and the smile followed

it. And one long day contained plenty of time to ru-
minate herself halfway to wacky. Eyes tearing up, she
pressed her lips together and struggled for control.
She was fierce with herself. *I am a strong woman. I can
do this!*

She glanced up at the silent television, and saw
an inebriated man throw his glass across the room to
shatter next to a woman's head. Their mouths gaped
wide, their nostrils flared, and their gestures were
brazen. Marca closed her eyes and lay back on her pillow, overcome with similar memories from her own
family. In her mind, she heard her parent's familiar
voices, yelling.

She hardly remembered her father's face, but
she recalled the caustic arguments between her parents that spanned her early years. In her mind, she
recalled everything that had happened, as if she were
still that little child.

Especially their final blow up.

Chapter 14

A few minutes after she heard the shower stop, five-year-old Marca peered around the corner. She always loved her parent's bedroom. The curtains were lacy white and matched the coverlet on the bed. It looked like a room a princess might have. Before she knew it, the sight drew her into the room.

She saw her mother, in her bathrobe, brushing her hair in front of the full length mirror on the back of her bathroom door. She hummed softly, one hand moving from her head to touch her abdomen, while she smiled. Marca suddenly felt good all over, and she hopped and jumped around in a circle, arms extended toward the ceiling and head thrown back.

Her mother laughed. "Come here, my dancing doll, *mi muñequita.*"

Marca ran around the bed and reached up. Her mother squatted down, and then knelt on the floor in front of her. She set aside the hairbrush and took Marca in both arms, looking into her face.

"*Mi'ja,*" she said. "I am thinking of our *família.* How would you like a little brother or sister?"

"A sister, *por favor,*" Marca said.

Her mother laughed, tossing back her hair. "It's a surprise, muñequita. We have to take what God sends us."

Marca looked at her with solemn eyes and nodded.

"It would be special to have another child in the family, *sí*? You, the big sister, could help me with the *bebé*."

"Sí, mamá."

Her mother laughed again, and squeezed Marca close.

Marca buried her nose in her mother's neck, and inhaled her special scent, mixed with the floral smell of the soap from the shower. She squeezed back with all her tiny strength, lost in the forever of that moment.

But the moment was cut short. Someone came through the front door, swinging it shut with too much force. He stumbled and cursed in Spanish.

"Quick now, mi'ja. Into your room. *Papá* may have had too much to drink again." Marca felt herself propelled out of her mother's room and directed towards her own.

Her mother walked past her toward the sounds in the living room. Marca listened from the doorway to her room, tensed for the blow of her father's yells. She heard her mother speak to him in her gentle voice, though her father responded, petulant like a child. But her mother's soothing tones seemed to reach him, and his voice became softer.

He sounded more like *Papacito* tonight, she decided, the one who set her in his lap and read her the comics from his laptop computer. He used a different voice for each character, and laughed when she giggled at his performance.

She tiptoed into the kitchen, where she could hear better, and sat on the floor behind the divider in the dark. From there, she could peek out at Mamá and Papá, and see whether she might be welcome to run out and gather up their hugs.

The living room was quiet. *Did they hear me leave my room?* She froze for several moments, and then dared to sneak just the top of her head out to where her eyes took in the view. She relaxed. They stood, entwined together, kissing.

"See?" Mamá said, pushing back from him just enough to look into his face. "Just leave that all behind. You are home now."

"Umm," he said, his mouth seeking hers again.

They made low contented sounds as they kissed. Then Papá cupped Sarita's bottom in his hands. She pushed away again and gave a laugh. "Don't you want some dinner first? You must be hungry after a hard day at work, *cara mia.*"

"Not what I'm hungry for," he said, but he let her move away.

"It's a special night. I have a surprise for you," she said, a little breathless. Tiny bounces emanating from her ankles, sent quivers up her body.

"Then dinner can wait," he said, reaching for her again. He tried to slip his hands inside her robe.

"Not that kind of surprise," she said, laughing and slapping away his hands in play. "It's better than that—it's wonderful news. Listen. We're having a bebé."

"*Qué?*" he asked, almost in a whisper.

"I'm pregnant. Marca won't be the only child any longer." She continued to smile, but Marca didn't like it as well as the happy bounce of a moment before. Mamá's face had lost something along with the laughter.

"Hell, Sarita, we can't afford another kid. I barely make enough to pay the bills as it is. And the crying last time was almost too much for me. You can't put me through that again—not with the pressure I'm under now. I'll go *loco*."

"Don't talk that way. A new life is a gift from God," she said. "You knew this could happen when we made love at that party. I warned you. When you didn't stop, I thought you were ready for our família to grow."

"I thought you were just afraid someone would walk in on us. I didn't understand. You have to get rid of it, before you get attached. I'm sorry, but there's no other way." His voice cajoled, but his face looked scared.

Her hands flew to her tummy. "This is not a misunderstanding, it is my bebé. And I am going to have this *hijo*, with you or without you." She spoke through her teeth.

His voice grew louder, approaching a yell. "Don't talk like I'm some villain. I had a good life before I married you. Now I work all the time, at a job I hate, all to get money for you and Marca. I gave up *todos*—everything for you!"

"Why is it always about money? If you quit drinking we'd have lots more money," she said, matching his volume.

"Don't you bring up my drinking. That's the price of keeping me sane in this house. Why don't you work if money's so damned *importante*?" He screamed the words, throwing his fists up in the air.

"And who would take care of *los hijos*? Our parents work, too. If I pay for childcare, it'll cost more than I can earn each week." Tears streamed down her face, and her nose ran. She swiped wildly at it, as if she really wanted to strike him.

"Well, you can just figure it out on your own. If you keep that bebé, I'm out of here. I've had it with you and all your demands. I can get a good *chinga* elsewhere. There's nothing else I want from you!"

"Then go. Go!" she bellowed.

Little Marca heard the front door slam, followed by the sound of her mother's bitter weeping. She had a lump in her throat. *Don't go, Papacito!*

* * *

It took years for Marca to learn that life wasn't defined by volatile interactions. Her family members blasted small matters into colossal episodes. She recognized the tendency in herself. They responded to each other's productions instinctively, caught up in the theater of the moment because there was something of love in it. Something pre-verbal.

Knowing she craved the wildness that passed for normal when she was young, Marca substituted dance, the rush of extreme sports like bungee jumping, or horror fiction. Over time, she practiced self-discipline until she could delay her reaction to adrenaline surges long enough to choose a positive resolution to most situations. Her family improved, too, though all went overboard now and then, especially when they were together over the holidays.

But now, her inability to care for herself triggered old reactions she thought she had laid to rest. Being waited on provoked guilt, and she feared she was taking on the old victim role her father had favored. She fretted, unable to concentrate on her work or the latest offering from Stephen King.

* * *

Anders stopped by after work to see how she fared. He carried a multi-colored mylar balloon with, "Get Well Soon!" written across it.

"Awful. Going mental. Afraid I'll endanger Lisa—and burden her. I need a distraction. Let me brainstorm on the case instead." She bit her tongue to keep from griping about minutiae, barely holding herself back.

"No worries—I understand. I'm a lousy patient, too, when I'm not well." He handed her the balloon, and she saw warmth in his expression. His smile made her duck her head as she spoke.

"Usually when I'm sick I stay away from people. I just submit—eat soup, sleep at all hours, curse to myself, and hide until I'm well again. But I'm so helpless without my leg. I can't even get around the house."

"Solving mysteries is my job," he said. "My supervisor teases me about my age, but really, I'm pretty good at it."

"At least tell me what's happened. Maybe that'll help. Has the kidnapper called Alice again?" She hoped the question made her sound less desperate for his company. But she didn't want him to leave.

"No, we're still waiting. But after our plans for tomorrow, I hope he'll quit worrying that you discovered his message and focus on the endgame—the ransom—instead."

"Terrific. I see you don't need my help." She barked a hollow laugh.

"Oh yes we do. I brought you something. Tim worked with the P.D. artist on a mockup of the man he saw by your house. Maybe you can identify him." He pulled a rolled paper out of his daypack. "Ta-duh," he said and flourished the rubber-banded scroll.

"I'll do my best, but I don't remember much about him."

"Maybe I can help boost your memory. Before I show you this, take a minute to concentrate on yesterday afternoon when the SUV hit you. Close your eyes and remember every detail of the incident. Ready?"

"Just a minute." She paused. "Yes." Her voice was softer.

"Okay. You leave the studio, look both ways, and step off the curb to cross the street. You see movement on the street. You bend down and reach out toward a spider. Do you see it in memory?"

"Yes. A male—with oversized pedipalps. Ironic that I got squashed while attempting to protect him."

"Keep your eyes closed. Tell me what happened next."

"I heard Lisa's yell and the roar of the SUV's engine at the same time. I glanced up. The vehicle grew larger as it bore down on me. I caught a glimpse of the man maneuvering it in my direction before I lunged sideways toward safety."

"Okay. Stop there. Bring the driver as clearly to mind as possible. Let me know when you are ready."

She paused again. "Okay. I'm ready."

Chapter 15

She heard a rustle of paper as Anders unrolled the artist's rendition. "Now. Open your eyes. Did he look like this man?"

She took her time and scrutinized the drawing before her, projecting onto it the indistinct face of her attacker. "I'm sorry, Anders, but this isn't the guy. I bet that screws up the case." Her shoulders drooped into a slump.

"No worries. Consider that one practice, okay? I want you to close your eyes again and let me know when you have the face of the driver back in mind. Run back through your memories again. No rush."

Her pause was shorter this time. "Now." She heard another swish of paper.

"Open your eyes. Did he look like this man?"

"Ye-es, yes. That's him. Wide-set eyes and messy, dark hair. The mouth isn't quite the same, but his lips were parted in the car. Wow, I remember more than I expected. But whose picture did you show me first?"

"Oh, that guy was from another case. I hoped, by seeing a contrast to the image in your mind, you might recall your attacker more clearly."

"Well, it worked. We have our man. So what next—his face on wanted posters?"

"The officers watching for him near the police station and the studio got a copy. But at Alice's request, you're the only other person who's seen it yet. She wants it kept secret until after she meets with the kidnapper. She's afraid he'll see it somehow and discover we are closing in on him."

"I understand. Oh, Anders, thank you so much. I feel better now—useful instead of helpless. I guess I really needed that. If you think of anything else I can do, I want to know, right away."

He leaned over and squeezed her shoulder, "You're a great help. If you want, when this case is over, we can spend some non-work time together—get to know each other better. What do you think?"

"I can't wait to feel less like an invalid, or especially, to spend time alone with you," she said. She grinned and wiggled her eyebrows at him. Then she laughed at her silliness. To her surprise, the laugh was authentic and made her feel better still.

* * *

The tall, dark-haired man moved quietly through the halls of the police department Sunday night, noting where lights indicated offices still in use. He veered away from those. He preferred not to explain his presence here at this hour. His feet stepped softly; he controlled his breathing.

At the nameplate, "Anders Johanson," next to the potted rubber tree, he glanced in both directions and then turned the knob. *No luck. Locked.* He didn't expect the mistakes of a newbie from Anders, but had to check just in case. He longed for those evidence reports Anders must have received by now. Just for re-assurance.

Most days, he held all the details under his power. The cremains had no DNA remaining in them, which made them impossible to identify. With Fyre's ring in the ashes, the coroner had to declare him dead, even if there were doubts. And once he issued the death certificate, the insurance company had to cough up the two million dollar claim.

That insurance claim was an unexpected bonus. He had only planned to ask for $500,000 in return for Fyre. Then he overheard the amount of the death benefit while he listened under the window at the Ruiz woman's house. Instinctively, he'd done the right thing in the instant that he decided to follow her home and see what he could find out about the cellphone. He had to admit, he was good at this.

He'd taken control of Mrs. Fyre, he was sure. She wanted her husband back so desperately that her telling a soul about his call to her was unlikely. *All mine. Wrapped around my pinky.*

True, the day Ruiz found the cellphone, he raged. And he failed to eliminate the potter—got so fired up that he hit her with that SUV out of his need to take action. Yet even that turned out well.

His careful habits protected him. He had rented the car several cities away, bolted on a purchased license plate, and returned the van the next day, un-marked, with the correct plate attached. By now, it had been cleaned, re-rented, and any remaining evidence that identified him, contaminated.

The attack may have been unnecessary. Ruiz might have recognized Mrs. Fyre's cellphone and re-turned it without eavesdropping on its recorded calls. Or Mrs. Fyre may have already erased his call, leaving the cell harmless. But since he couldn't be certain, he had gone and checked it out.

Breaking into Ruiz's house, while she was away, had been ridiculously easy. Her backyard was fenced, and no other house had a direct view of its back door. He wore a cap and a workman's shirt just in case he was seen. But he'd removed the glass from that window within 60 seconds, reached in, and clicked open the locks.

When he called the phone number, he heard no ringtone, but it could have been turned off. His gloves left no sign of his search for the cell. He was careful, but thorough. It was not inside the house—he made certain of that. Then he prepped the frame, installed a new window, relocked the door, and carried away the waste like an experienced glazier. He doubted anyone noticed him or the new glass.

He called Mrs. Fyre the following day. He needed certainty that his plan was safe. And she answered; so he knew she had gotten back her cellphone.

Since Ruiz held the phone for such a short time, he knew the chance that she had heard his call was miniscule. Still, she was his biggest question mark—a variable he had not anticipated. *Crap.*

He wouldn't allow her to damage his preparation. His focus had settled on Johanson and Ruiz, the two possible troublemakers, and he intended it to stay there.

Turning now, he traveled down the dark hallway to an exit. All was well; he was sure of it. The lab reports only meant extra peace of mind. But since that damn Ruiz had surprised him, he'd try again another night.

Nobody was perfect, but he was close. And it was his turn to grab some luck. He'd make sure of it.

* * *

Matthew observed that Enemy left during the day—possibly worked nearby. After retreating upstairs, he was gone for hours. *He's gone at night, too.*

Once he knew Enemy had left him alone, Matthew fingered as much of the left top edge of the box as possible using his limited range of motion. He worked to extend his reach each time. So far, he had explored one hinge.

Part two of his daily training cycle followed his exercise routine. He grated his chain against the hinge. Always, he ground the same link at the same point, and deliberately kept from marring the wood. Hinge-grinding lasted two hours at a stretch, and he counted seconds to minutes to hours and kept track. *If I'm here long enough, either the hinge or the chain will give way. It's inevitable.*

His wrists cramped with the effort, but he was committed to his plan. By causing no visible damage to his hands, he hid his efforts from Enemy's notice. The pain represented progress to him. And it reminded him that he still had choices, even locked in a coffin.

Chapter 16

Anders thumbed through the evidence Tuesday morning as he had done each day since assigned to the case, searching for new insight and insuring he forgot nothing. Only a small bit of information was new.

No crematoria within one-hundred-miles of Woodsdale reported a theft of remains. Instead, most had a registry of cremains never collected. Some stored hundreds of cremation urns that had been abandoned, probably because families couldn't afford to pay the costs. Each facility reported that they had double-checked their storage areas, as requested, and ensured that all remains were accounted for.

He heard a cellphone sing in a nearby office, and set down the report. Jessica St. Marie tiptoed in and gave Anders thumbs up, pointed to the cellphone, and sat down beside him. The phone was set on speaker. Anders activated the trace.

The altered voice sounded eerie, like an alien creature speaking through a computer-translator on the other end of the line. He imagined a slimy-skinned monster from an old science fiction movie. His skin crawled.

"Today's the big day," the voice said. "Our exchange will take place at 3:00 at Woodsdale Train Station near the ferry. Bring the cash in the smallest backpack that will hold it—unmarked bills with nonconsecutive serial numbers only. Come alone and wait inside the station. No police involvement will be tolerated. You'll receive your next instructions there. Do you understand?"

"Yes. Untraceable cash in a backpack. Wait inside the train station at 3:00 p.m. today," St. Marie said.

"I guarantee that you will see your husband before the exchange to prove that he is still alive and that I have not harmed him."

"I understand. Thank you."

"Tell nobody about this call, and erase it immediately after I hang up."

"I will." She took a breath as if she was about to speak again. Instead, a click sounded from the phone and she set it down. "He hung up."

"That was quick," Anders said. "No chance of a trace. But we have all we need: the meeting place and time. And loads to do before then."

* * *

Anders had checked and rechecked his arrangements well ahead of the kidnapper's call. A police team, formed especially for the handoff, had awaited only the time, date and location to initiate their counter plan. He set their strategy in motion with a call.

Starting an hour ahead of time, and arriving at various points up until the hand-off, police officers disguised as ordinary citizens would involve themselves in everyday activities around the Woodsdale

Railway Station. A gray-haired man would bird-watch from the senior center parking lot on the beach side of Railroad Ave. He would sit on a swivel chair—binoculars in hand, notebook and bird identification guide in his lap—and play lookout, alternately scanning the beach behind him through a gap between buildings, and the hills beyond the station, viewing all access routes to the station along the way.

Jessica St. Marie and another young officer, in street clothes, would pose as lovers leaning against a telephone pole on the sidewalk two blocks up Railroad Ave., wrapped in one another's arms. Another officer would wait in his car at the front of the ferry loading area facing Main Street. Peter Landsbury, in a business suit, would enjoy savory chicken tandoori at the Indian buffet between the waiting traffic and the ferry dock south of Main Street. A homeless man, Benjamin Mulback, one hand lying atop a hijacked shopping basket filled with life possessions in garbage bags, would nap on a bench outside the train station, snoring every few breaths.

Anders was certain that the police would be well camouflaged but ready for anything. The suspect would not be leaving the train station with Matthew Fyre. He'd be leaving in handcuffs for a long stay behind bars.

* * *

Alice had packed two million dollars cash into a backpack as the suspect instructed. She let the police put a GPS beacon into the sole of her shoe and a bulletproof vest under her jacket, but she refused to wear a camera or wire. *Whatever else the police feel they need to do around me, I choose to play this straight.* The less she had to cover up when she spoke to the suspect, the less likelihood she'd make a mistake.

As 3:00 p.m. approached, she parked her car at the seaside park just northeast of the ferry dock, where there was free parking, and with the pack slung over one shoulder, crossed Main St. and walked southeast along Railroad Ave. to the station. Pausing outside, she checked the time on her cellphone, took a deep breath, pulled open the front door, and entered. Inside, a few people moved about. Only the man behind the ticket counter looked up. She made her mouth give him a brief smile in passing. Her eyes did not smile. They watched.

She had never seen her husband's kidnapper, but had studied the mockup drawing Tim helped design. Holding that image in mind, her gaze scanned every face in sight. Nobody she saw resembled the picture.

As instructed, she sat on a bench and waited. She gave herself a pep talk that kept her mind focused on success. *I'm afraid, but that's okay. Who wouldn't be? For Matthew, I can do this. No problem.*

After about five minutes, a woman entered, cash gripped in one hand, and discussed various trains and fares with the ticket seller. Alice glanced at her and away. She had requested not to know which people in the area were police, though they supposedly covered the area. She felt better telling the truth about them, but a part of her wanted the comfort of knowing who they were.

After five more minutes, a man stepped unobtrusively through the rear door from the train tracks. He took low, careful steps, his body unnaturally still except for his feet. She almost didn't recognize him. But a familiar head movement drew her eye like fireworks on the Fourth. He couldn't subdue his signature movements enough for her to miss them.

Matthew had lost weight and his skin was pallid. His normally kempt hair was plastered to his head with grease where it didn't stick up in a cowlick, and his clothes looked slept in.

She jumped up. "Matthew!"

He saw her, but his eyes went wide. He walked forward slowly, his expression full of longing, but his palms extended as if he pushed her back.

"Don't hug me, please, sweetheart. I'm wired," he said, and lifted his shirttail with intense delicacy.

At first she thought that his abductor listened via microphone to their conversation. Then his shirt exposed the bulging belt of explosives around his midriff, wired to detonate. She gasped. A wave of vertigo hit her like a tsunami. She staggered and had to catch her balance, hands on her thighs.

"Oh no, Matthew. No."

He lowered his shirt down over the belt, wincing, and then stopped several feet from her. "I need to trade backpacks with you, honey, then walk away alone, back to the kidnapper. He says he'll let me go once he gets the money, but please don't trust him. I think he's lying. I'm afraid," he stopped and swallowed, "that I may not see you again."

"Don't say that. Let's hope for the best."

"Please, don't come after us—you can't rescue me from this." He looked down at his midsection.

"Where is he?"

"Driving around the area, I think. He doesn't take chances. He told me to cut across to Sunset, and then walk up Dayton until he meets me.

"Stay safe, sweetheart. I couldn't stand to lose you. You are, and have always been, the meaning in my life."

She realized he was saying goodbye, and a pit opened in her stomach. Sweat stood out on Matthew's forehead, and she heard his rapid breathing. He held out his pack, and they traded. She touched his ice-cold fingers as if accidently. He hesitated, prolonging the contact. It was a caress.

"I'll be cautious, I promise. Hurry back, my sweet man. I won't give up on you. Not ever." She didn't take her eyes from his.

"I'll try. I love you." His voice dropped to a husky whisper.

"I love you too, Matthew, whatever happens. Be safe." She kissed the tips of her first two fingers and held them out to him. He kissed his fingers and touched them to hers. Then each touched fingers to lips.

Matthew turned back to the rear door. Still stepping like the floor was thin ice, he pushed it open and left. He didn't look back.

She tried to remain where she stood, chin quivering, but the cord of her affection for Matthew drew her toward the rear doors. She traced his progress across the train track and to the right, as he angled obliquely southeast from the station.

The woman who had purchased the train ticket brushed past her and stepped out by the tracks, looking both ways as if she didn't know from which direction the train might arrive. The contact awakened Alice, as if from a trance, and she remembered her promise. She stepped to where she could see out the back door while creating a lesser target. She pressed her body close against the inner wall and glanced out the front windows for a moment before she looked through the back at Matthew's receding figure.

The homeless man, who had dozed on the front bench, now pushed his cart down Railroad Avenue towards Dayton, gesturing to himself as if holding a heated conversation with God. The two lovers, arms wound about each other's waists, stood at the front doors of the station kissing and giggling. They seemed to have eyes for nobody else, but the man might be watching Matthew past the woman's face. The woman, she realized, was Jessica St. Marie. Alice swallowed and looked away.

She waited, watching. Matthew approached Sunset, a block from the station. She viewed him across the empty land adjoining the tracks. A man in a business suit, who held a newspaper, walked toward Matthew without looking his way— approaching the same corner of Sunset Avenue, but from Main Street. He walked briskly. The contrast between their gaits was enormous, and it appeared he would reach Matthew just as Matthew stepped onto the sidewalk.

Thinking again of the explosives her husband wore, she grimaced. *I hope that guy isn't a policeman— that he doesn't grab Matthew suddenly.* But she also wished the police knew which streets Matthew planned to walk so they might rescue him.

She glanced around again, her mind flitting like a hummingbird. She hoped all the people near her were cops. She hoped none of them were. She hoped they'd liberate him. She hoped they wouldn't try. Her heart thudded in her ears, louder than the sounds nearby. She thought it might drive her mad.

Suddenly, a police car turned left from Dayton onto Sunset and stopped at the curb in front of Matthew, even though it faced into traffic on his side of the street. He handed the backpack through the window and then climbed into the back seat. As quickly as it had appeared, the car U-turned and disappeared back down Dayton, the way it had come. The businessman stopped abruptly as he stepped into Matthew's footprints of a moment before. His face turned toward the vanishing car. She recognized Peter Landsbury.

Hand to her face, Alice discovered she held her breath, and released it. *They rescued him. Oh my God,*

the police saved him. If they can only diffuse the bomb—?
She shuddered, hope and fear clashing painfully inside her chest. Her stomach ached. Her field of vision tunneled narrower, blotches blocking part of what remained. She braced one hand against the back of a chair, lowered her head, and took a deep breath.

Straightening, she looked around again. The couple no longer kissed. They stood further down the sidewalk, looking more like cops and less like lovers. One spoke into a radio. Across the street behind her, the bird-watching senior had lowered his binoculars and left his chair. He also spoke via radio and then crossed toward the station. She went out the front door and heard radio chatter in the air.

"Are you a police officer?" she asked. "Please tell me what's happening. What should I do next?"

The senior turned to her. "Stay inside and wait, just in case the suspect retaliates. We don't know his location right now, but we doubt it's inside the railway station. He could appear from anywhere. As long as he is unaccounted for, you are in potential danger.

"We're determining which officer picked up your husband. When he can pause to answer his radio, we'll tell you where you may meet them."

Concerns avalanched from her mouth. "Matthew had a bomb strapped to him. Can the officer in his car disarm it? What if it detonates by remote control? Could it go off inadvertently?"

"I'm sure he informed the officer of the bomb right away. It had to be his biggest concern. We probably haven't raised the officer on the radio yet, because he has to make sure the suspect isn't following. Once he stops, he'll need all his attention to defuse that bomb. Explosives work takes concentrated effort. He can call in a specialist if he needs to.

"So wait inside, please. I'm sure we'll know more soon. I'll keep you informed."

She went back inside the train station, her stomach roiling. All the glass she had looked through in the front and back of the building seemed suddenly unsafe. *Something's not right. I heard it in his tone. Oh, Matthew.*

She returned to where she stood when she watched Matthew slip into the police car. There was nothing left to see. The car was gone. The businessman had vanished. The sidewalk was empty. She took a deep breath, let it out, then chose a seat where she could see out both sets of doors: front and back.

When she leaned over to set the daypack on the floor, she realized it was heavy—far too heavy to be empty. Her breath came faster. With darting fingers, she fumbled open the top and reached inside. She pulled out wad after wad of local newspaper, then a brick, and finally a DVD in a jewel-box case. Turning over the DVD, she could see that it was no commercial release. It was unlabeled. She jumped up and sprinted out the front door, waving the DVD in the air, the daypack forgotten, sitting on the station floor.

Out front, she shoved the DVD at the senior officer and snapped out her words in a rapid jumble. "I found this in the pack Matthew traded me for the money. It must be a message from the kidnapper. I need to see it immediately! Find me a computer right now!" Her voice ended in a squeak.

The officer, clearly distracted, took what she pushed into his hands, but didn't seem to see it. He put the forefinger of one hand against his ear as if listening, and held up a finger on the hand holding the disk to silence her. His eyes were unfocused, his brow wrinkled in concentration.

Alice's teeth clenched tight as her heart raced. She bit her tongue trying not to interrupt and ask what was happening. Although she wasn't a religious person, her gut urged her to kneel and pray. She resisted, but she could tell that whatever the officer listened to was information essential to Matthew's fate.

"Mrs. Fyre," he said, at last making eye contact with Alice. "The patrol car that picked up your husband came from the Police Department's vehicle pool, but we have no record of any officer signing it out. The driver neither responded to his radio nor showed up at the department with your husband. Instead, he vanished. All officers involved in the operation have reported in from their locations.

"We believe that the kidnapper deceived us all. Somehow, he obtained a police cruiser, and he used it to surprise us into taking no action against him.

"Meanwhile, he took your husband captive once again."

Chapter 17

Matthew realized that he had lost his equilibrium. Enemy refused to release him after receiving the insurance benefit, just like he warned his wife. But once he saw Alice, his desire for her—for their life together—overwhelmed him. He dared hope that he might go free, visualized returning to her, squeezing her tight. Now he cursed into the silence, remembering the events of the afternoon. *Damn it, I knew better.*

* * *

When the police car pulled up beside him, Matthew thought he was finally safe. But he saw Enemy's stocking mask when he passed the daypack through the window and realized the deception. Because he wore the bomb belt, he recognized that no alternative to his fate existed. So he climbed into the backseat.

Enemy threw him the black blindfold he wore on the way to the train station. "Put that back on." Then he raised the bulletproof panel between the front and back seats. He ignored Fyre for the remainder of the drive.

Matthew let the blindfold gap as much as he reasonably could. He saw a strip of his lap when he looked down, and one of the roof of the car, above. *Better than nothing.* He counted the turns and estimated the distance between them, creating a map inside his head until too many details crowded his mind, and the map disintegrated.

Why keep me? He has his money now. Only one answer held any hope—Enemy needed an opportunity to count it—make certain he had not been deceived. A long shot, of course, but no other reason boded well for Matthew, so he kept it foremost in his mind.

At every bump and jostle of the car he tensed, anticipating his atoms exploding across the universe. *Relax. Enemy wants to survive this drive, too.* At least, he hoped that was true.

After thirteen minutes, Enemy pulled off onto a surface that crunched like gravel. Matthew recognized the sound beneath the tires, and he twisted his face into a grimace. He heard an automatic garage door open. The car stopped, and the garage door ground closed. He waited in the backseat with the blindfold in place until Enemy opened a side door, but his shoulders slumped.

"Get out!"

He confirmed that this was his old prison before he had passed through the two doors that framed the stairway up from the garage. The house smelled like his grave. At the second flight of stairs, he stepped down, willing his leaden feet to lift. The toe of his left shoe dragged and he lost his balance, but grabbed the rail before he crashed down the flight, and then took the stairs using more care.

"Take off the blindfold and get in the box!"

"I still have the belt on," he said, but stepped into the box.

"It stays on until you're cuffed. Lay down. Arms up!"

He raised his arms and watched the cuffs re-encircle his wrists. *Trapped again.*

"Feet up! Legs spread!"

Matthew revisited mental scenarios where he stole control from Enemy during this changeover. But none appeared reasonable while he wore explosives. He fumed, ready to take action.

Enemy cuffed his ankles and secured the cord that connected his limbs. Matthew lowered his legs.

"Get out."

His lower back protested the familiar stoop of the cord that bent him forward. The extra weight of the belt accentuated his discomfort.

"Spread your hands and feet wide, and lean against the table, back to me." Enemy followed and removed the belt after fumbling behind Matthew, probably to disarm it.

"Back in the box."

"I'm thirsty."

Enemy screamed. "Get back in the box now and shut your mouth!" His neck turned scarlet.

Well, I tried. Matthew returned to the coffin and repeated raising his feet and hands as Enemy removed the cable. *Still can't take him, damn it.*

The door to the box slammed down, and he heard the too-familiar snick of the lock. His eyes blinked away dust. His ears rang.

He listened until he heard Enemy leave. The entire trip from the car had taken mere minutes.

* * *

He gulped air, held it, and then released his breath along with the tightness of his frame. He let the terror of the explosives ease away. He didn't dwell on alternate scenarios. The past was behind him. Instead, he started his exercise routine, the familiarity of the actions calming him more than his deep breath.

When he reached the place where he grated chain against hinge, he wondered whether the effort would pay off. His glimpse of freedom had passed. The hourglass of his life was running low on sand.

* * *

Alice endured the train station for a quarter-hour longer before she decided to return to her car, police or no. As she stepped out the front door of the railroad station, the senior officer stepped up beside her.

"May I escort you?"

"Do what you want. Nobody in your department listens to me anyway. We should have done this my way. You just lost me my husband. So now what, huh?"

"Detective Johanson called a strategy meeting as soon as we get back. We'll know more after that. You can check with him later."

Alice steamed. These might be Anders's orders, for all she knew, but the officer's words removed her from the crime fighters' team and placed her squarely back into the role of civilian. *Not gonna happen.*

"I'll be at that meeting," she said. "So you can give me back my DVD." She stopped and held out her hand.

The senior officer hesitated, but after a glance at her face, he pulled it out from inside his coat and held it out it to her. She grabbed it out of his hands and gripped it so tightly that the case bowed inward.

"I'm fully aware that Matthew's chances for survival just dropped big time; there's no need to protect me from that fact," she said between clenched teeth. "It's clear: the kidnapper has the money and little reason to keep Matthew alive. And you don't know where to find them.

"If you don't bring him back to me alive, I'm going to call every news station from here to Portland and tell them what a bunch of incompetent, inept, irresponsible pigs you are. Your stupidity better not have cost Matthew his life!"

The officer stepped back from her, his eyes opening wide as she continued.

"Understand this: I am part of this investigation for the long haul. I cannot—I shall not—give up on my husband."

* * *

The kidnapper drove the police car straight from the house where he stashed Matthew to a detailing company. He drew a knitted cap down over his hair, slipped an appliance into his mouth that changed his jaw line, and added a slight limp as he entered the door. He spoke at a slower pace, his voice pitched higher than usual. He affected an Old South enunciation, and he addressed the man at the main desk.

"Hi, y'all. I called about having a police car detailed," he drawled, his final tone rising as if he asked a question.

"Yes sir. We can take it right in. What level of detailing do you want done?" The fellow outlined a deep flow of money as he enthusiastically described the company's top options.

"It's a surprise for Detective Johanson who's out of town. When he returns tomorrow, we'd like you to give a call saying his car is all spiffed up like new. Kind of a thank you for his good work, you know."

He chose the company's top interior option, paid in cash, and gave a false name. Instead of his number, he gave Johanson's phone extension. "Here's a little extra for doing a thorough job and calling the detective in the morning. He'll be so pleased."

He imagined Johanson's confusion when the call came in, and smiled. He wished he could be there and see it happen. The detailed car would tell Johanson exactly what type of a cop he was. *An amateur, just like the older guys say.*

Since he chose the top detailing option, he received a complementary ride back to a place of his choice—a block from where he parked his own car, four blocks from the police station. On the seat beside him, he set a small suitcase he had carried along to the detailer's shop. His work clothes were inside. He checked the time on his cellphone—nearly 4:30 p.m. He better return to work for an hour. *Don't want to draw undesired attention. Later, I'll figure out what to do about the prisoner—if anything.*

* * *

At the P.D., Anders watched angry cops gather as he hooked a projector to his computer, and loaded the DVD.

Alice stood beside him, her arms on her hips. She hissed at him. "Hurry up! Forget the stupid projector! You're wasting time!"

"I stood within a yard of him," Peter told the other cops, "when he climbed into that squad car."

"I had my piece on me," said Benjamin. "Could've shot out the tires, but didn't see a reason."

"I put an APB out on the cruiser," Anders said, as he stood. "Somebody might sight it, unless he hid it in a hurry."

"Face it. You guys screwed this up, just like I figured you would!" Alice snapped. "The suspect demanded there be no police involvement. But your detective, here, wouldn't let me do it any other way."

She stabbed her forefinger into the air in Ander's direction.

Anders ignored her outburst. "Attention, everyone. The backpack Matthew traded for the ransom contained a DVD that Alice passed on to me. I hooked up this projector so we can watch it together. Is everyone here?" He paused and scanned the room. "Study it for clues. Let's learn all we can about this guy." He flicked off the lights, and tapped a key on his laptop before anyone else could speak up.

The video projected onto the wall. Anders hit the arrow to start it playing.

A figure sat in a chair behind a small table, an unfinished dirt wall framing him from behind. He wore a white tee shirt, but the tabletop blocked the view of his lower half. A stocking masked his face, he had on a Seattle Mariner's baseball cap, and his hands wore garden gloves sporting a ladybug design. When he spoke, his voice sounded alien—just as it had on Alice's cellphone.

"Greetings, Mrs. Fyre. In a few minutes, I leave for the train station to accept your payment in return for your husband. By the time you view this video the exchange will have concluded.

"You chose its success or failure. If you involved the police, your husband suffers now. If you did as I asked, he is safe beside you.

"If you chose to follow my directions in detail, consider this video my thanks for your cooperation and my good-bye. It has been a pleasure dealing with you. I doubt our paths will cross again.

"If you caved, and involved the police, you cannot rectify your miscalculation. I will not be handled. You will hear from me soon about the consequences.

"By the way, the police cruiser I borrowed will be back in police hands in less than 24 hours. Don't bother to tell them, though. Soon enough, they will know. It can be our little surprise, okay?

"Good day, Mrs. Fyre."

Silence padded the room for several seconds after the video ended.

Then Alice sank into a chair. "Oh my God. So he did find out about the police screwing with this operation. My poor Matthew."

Anders slugged one fist into the other hand. Then he spoke in a strong voice. "We don't know that for certain. This guy is smart, always a step ahead of us. He made sure he had an angle. He knows how we think—depended on our assumptions for his getaway strategy, just in case we were looking on.

"If we're going to catch him at the next opportunity, we've got to snake inside his mind in the same way. So what did you get from the vid?" Anders asked.

"Following a ransom, the victim is either released or murdered. I assume that he's planned Matthew's death." The senior cop turned to Alice and added, "Sorry to speak so plainly, ma'am, but that's fact."

"I know." She swallowed hard, and then continued. "He contacted me by phone in the past, so I expect he will again."

"I concur. What else. Anyone."

"That unfinished cellar must be in an old structure. If we check the age of housing developments, we'll discover where root cellars were constructed. Canvass those areas using the drawing," Jessica said.

"Excellent idea. The traced call came from the ferry dock, and the transfer happened at the train station. Good chance the suspect is local, or works in the area. He stashed his victim in town, I'd wager," said Anders. "Volunteers who can research housing immediately?" the detective asked.

Hands went up, and he chose the senior cop and Peter. "Get out there and knock doors tonight. Keep me informed."

"I appreciate getting back onto this case. I can canvass the area around the train station," Benjamin said. "See if anyone knows anything worthwhile."

"The sooner you get out there, the better," Anders said. "You help him." He nodded to the cop from the ferry line.

"Any leads on the SUV that hit Ms. Ruiz?" Peter asked.

"Negative. The license plate number led to a thrift shop that resells dozens of used license plates. Their employees don't remember who bought plates, and we can't pinpoint when they were purchased. Possibly months ago."

"Figures," Benjamin muttered.

"Several rental agencies feature the black Chevy Tahoe as their primary SUV in its size category," Anders said. "Four agencies at the airport rent them plus others in neighboring cities. We searched their SUV's on lot for trace evidence and questioned the renters who drove them. Nothing connects them to the crime. However, we still await the return of some longer-term rentals that might contain evidence.

"In addition to rental agencies, sellers of Chevys in the area supplied us with lists of purchasers. We questioned them all. They all say the vehicles were in their possession at the time of the assault against Marca. No evidence leads us to assume otherwise.

"If our canvassing doesn't pan out, we'll re-interview people we spoke to previously. We can now show our drawing to employees at Goodwill, SUV suppliers, and people living near the pottery studio. Then we widen our search parameters. Legwork may solve the case. If anything else occurs to you, please get in touch right away. Let's do this."

He saw Alice Fyre start the video again, while the officers took off on their follow-up activities. She had done the same with the first phone message, played it over and over.

Although the meeting had concluded with a call to action, the quick passage of time left a fog of disquiet hanging in the air like stale cigar smoke.

Chapter 18

"How goes the investigation?" Marca asked Anders when he called her from his office during his takeout meal that night. "Any new leads?"

"Nothing, and we need a quick breakthrough, so I'm working through dinner. Even now, Matthew may be dying, for all we know. There is no reason I can imagine, short of further extortion, for the suspect to keep Matthew alive, now that he has the insurance money. Hostages become more problematic as time passes. The need to dispose of them intensifies, so that the kidnapper can escape the scene of the crime and move on."

"Tell me what you know. Maybe a new set of ears will hear things differently."

He shared the information from the meeting earlier in the day. "Not one of us suspected that the suspect was driving when Matthew climbed into the police car. Clearly, we were all kicking ourselves for being deceived.

"This afternoon, officers canvassed the area around the train station in case locals saw something we missed. I'm about to read through the interviews. Hopefully, something we overlooked will jump out at me."

Marca thought about the clues and evidence in detail. "I need to sleep on all this. Sometimes when I wake up I have unique ah-ha's. Right now, it sounds like you've done all you can. But I appreciate you giving my brain something to focus on besides my stupid leg."

"It's great that I can bounce ideas off of you. A non-police insight can be very helpful." His voice was warm.

He sounds so affectionate. A professional but also a sweetie. I can't wait to see more of him, in more ways than one.

"Any time," Marca said aloud. "Thanks for the call. It's great to hear your voice. Just what the doctor would've ordered, if I were the doctor." She gave a short laugh at herself, and he joined in.

* * *

In the morning, Anders found info on his voicemail that another black Chevy Tahoe SUV, rented from a city north of Woodsdale before the assault on Marca, had been returned by its subsequent renter. He had Ana send out her assistant to collect any data that might have survived.

He asked the manager about who worked the desk the day the SUV was rented. That person would be at work in the morning, so he made an appointment to show her the art reconstruction.

* * *

Later that morning, a call came to his desk phone that confused Anders at first. "You want me to do what? But I didn't bring in my cruiser to be detailed. I'm sure you have the wrong officer."

"A man dropped it off yesterday as a surprise for you," said the assured voice of the employee on the other end of the line. "He left your name and number with a request that we call you as soon as it was ready.

"He explained that he had to return the keys to the police department vehicle pool, so that you would have them today, so he left the car unlocked for us. We kept it inside the garage where it would stay safe. It's time to move another vehicle into that dock now. So if you could pick it up as soon as possible—."

Abruptly, he realized which car it must be. "Hold on a minute." Setting down the phone, he popped down the hall to Jessica St. Marie's office. "What was the license plate of the cruiser stolen yesterday?"

When he returned to the phone, he read off the number.

"Yep. That's the car." She sounded much cheerier.

"I'll be over in half an hour." Under his breath, he cursed the suspect's ingenuity. He speed-dialed Ana.

"Ana? Believe it or not, a car turned up, in addition to that rental, which might yield evidence."

"Man! Such a hurry. Not one sweet word for me before you launch into business?" She made her voice deep and sulky.

"You know I always think of you, babe—I called, didn't I? But I need to pick up a police cruiser, stolen from us, used in the crime, and then detailed afterward. I'll need to check it for booby-traps before I drive it. The explosive belt Matthew was wearing was a warning of what this guy is knowledgeable about.

Will you come along and make sure I don't contaminate the car any further than necessary?"

"I'll do better than that. I'll drive it back here for you. I have disposables I can bring so I can suit up once we arrive.

"We'll confiscate the detailer's trash bags, too. Whatever they vacuumed out of that squad car will be inside one of them. But the bags are filthy things that could easily contaminate a detailed vehicle. It would never do to carry them inside of it. I think we should stash them in your cruiser, sweetheart, and you can drive them back here for analysis. You can play garbage man for me."

* * *

Marca felt much more human the next morning after her talk with Anders. He always made her feel better. She stopped her mind from ruminating on her situation by turning it to him, and was able to relax with Stephen King for a couple of hours after brunch.

But in the early afternoon, she heard sounds down on the main floor that seemed unusual, from her limited experience in Lisa's house. First, a thud sounded against a downstairs window. *A bird?*

She got off of the bed where she had been reading, grabbed her crutches, and clumped to various windows on the second floor, looking for a hurt bird on the ground. She realized that from the angle of an upstairs window, she could not quite see what lay against the outside wall of the house.

She considered braving the stairs for a closer look but thought better of it. *Stomping around to upstairs windows made my stupid leg throb already.* So she climbed back into bed and propped it up on its pillow.

After resting a minute to let the pain ease to a bearable level, she picked up her novel. As the book began to catch her interest again, she heard a more alarming sound. The front doorknob rattled, and a few minutes later, the back knob. She froze at first, not sure what to do. Then she called Anders.

"I'm afraid that somebody is breaking into Lisa's house!"

"Get out of there right now!"

"I can't! I'm too slow on crutches. I'd be too obvious."

"Then hide. I'll call 911. Then I'll be there as fast as I can drive."

"I'll try," she said. "But where could I go except into a closet with this leg?"

"A closet sounds fine. It should gain us a little time."

"Okay. Hurry!"

She hoisted herself back off the bed, her heart pulsing so hard she felt the beat in her throat. It thudded like taiko drums in her ears. Even her eyes seemed to throb to its rhythm.

She limped down the hallway again on her crutches, more quickly this time, ignoring the pain as she searched for decent concealment. At the top of the stairs was a full bathroom decorated in aqua tones. The door had a flimsy interior lock—the child-safe type that could be opened from outside with the poke of a screwdriver into the knob. After a quick look inside, she turned it down as a hiding place. *Too obvious.* But she twisted the lock on the door and pulled it shut. *Maybe that will slow him down for a moment or two.*

Quick glances into the other rooms yielded no better hiding places. After pulling their doors closed, she decided on the closet in Lisa's bedroom, where the bed was made, rather than in her own, where she had lain in the crumpled sheets only minutes before. He would probably check that room first.

As she pushed through clothes to the rear of the closet, she heard the back door crash as if it had just been forced open. Stifling a cry, she crouched into the back corner of the closet, broken leg extended along the back wall, one hand braced against the wall near the corner. She trembled, crutches held loosely in her other hand, trying to make herself tiny. Her shaking wouldn't obey her attempt to stop it. She thought she should form a plan in case he found her, but her mind turned to fog.

Oh God oh God oh God.

Chapter 19

Anders grabbed his Glock from his drawer, stuffed it into the shoulder holster and slipped into his suit jacket. He sprinted to his car, fumbling the cellphone from his pocket and hitting the speed-dial for 911 in mid-stride. They answered as he climbed in, and he ordered an emergency vehicle with an EMT and an armed responder to Lisa's address.

He had his car moving before he hung up or buckled his seatbelt. Turning out of the parking lot, he sped forward. Siren blaring, he hit the horn and swerved around vehicles that didn't pull over swiftly enough, always on the outlook for pedestrians, as he flew along the Woodsdale streets. *This is all my fault. I told Marca to stay with a friend, and now she's in danger.*

He didn't know what he'd find when he arrived, but he depended on the EMT to reach Marca before he could. *Damn. This is taking too long!* His tires screeched as he slid to an abrupt stop for cross traffic. *Move. Move. Move!* Then he was through the cross street and back up to speed.

* * *

After the crash of the back door, Marca heard no sound for several minutes. *Did he leave? Is he searching downstairs?*

She tried to extend her hearing and found she was holding her breath. Exhaling through her mouth, she forced herself to gulp silent, even breaths as she listened.

The creak of a step made her jump. *Was that him?* She stretched her eyes wide, willing herself to generate x-ray vision, like Superman's. The closet door and walls blinded her. Her heart thumped louder.

The knob on the front bathroom door rattled. "I'm coming for youuu," a voice teased in a sing-song tone.

Her worst fears were confirmed by his words. *This is no ordinary break in. He's coming for me!*

"Then he barked, "Open the door!" There was a pause, and then a crunch as the bathroom door slammed open.

She gasped as she heard the shower curtain ripped down. An angry sound, that might have been a curse, followed.

She heard his heavy stomping, then something heavy crashed. She heard the closet door open in the office next door to the bathroom.

Footfalls in the hall approached the two bedrooms at her end of the floor. She opened her mouth and attempted to pant without sound as she adjusted the clothes that hung in front of her into a better screen.

He entered her bedroom next, his movements noisy. She heard her bed scrape along the floor, the closet bang open and hangers clatter. Then the door to her shower thudded, glass shattering as he smashed it shut.

Moments later he was in Lisa's bedroom just feet from where she hid. She shook, and bit her lip, fighting a whimper. *Where is Anders?*

"You think you can hide from me, Marca Ruiz, but it's hopeless. I know what you did, and I'll enjoy making you pay for it." The bed screeched along the floor.

"That bastard's wife? Alice? You listened to her cellphone messages, *private* messages. Then you went to the police like an idiot. I should have killed you when I was in your hospital room!"

He was in my hospital room? And how did he find me here? Panic pierced her. *I'm not safe anywhere!*

The door of the closet jerked open, and large feet in hiking boots blocked her exit. Despite the clothes between them, he reached in and grabbed her arm as if she was the only thing inside. He jerked her up and toward him before she could get her crutches braced beneath her. One fell from her hand.

"No!" Marca screamed. "Get out! I called the police. They're on the way."

She took huge one-footed hops forward, attempting to stay upright where she had a chance to engage the man. *He's tall. His arms are too long.* Her good leg stumbled over a pair of shoes, and she fell with a scream.

She grunted as she slammed into the hardwood floor, the breath knocked out of her. Agony shot up her broken leg. Through wet eyes she saw his dark hair and flat, twisted features inside his stocking mask as he bent to reach for the arm that her fall had torn from his fingers. She yanked it away. As she finally managed to take a breath, the smell of stale sausage came to her on his breath, and she struggled not to gag.

She still held one crutch, her last hope, and she flung it forward, lance-like, with all of her remaining strength. She aimed for the man's kneecap.

Effortlessly, he caught the crutch in midair. Then, with a roar, he heaved it across the room. The full-length mirror exploded into a million splinters. He dragged her free of the closet, yelling at her.

"You little bitch. You think that leg hurts now? Just wait until I'm done with you! It'll be nothing but background noise."

She clawed at his arm with her free hand, gasping through her pain, but ready to bite if he drew her close enough.

A siren grew loud, stopped, and a car door opened and then slammed shut in the driveway below.

"See? They're here," Marca said, and let out a yell. "Up here! Help me! Help!"

The man spun around, growling like a caged beast. He turned back long enough to aim a wicked kick at her side, and then he dashed for the stairs. She lay where she fell, mouth open like a fish left behind by the waves, again unable to draw in oxygen as this new pain flooded through her.

A moment later, a deep voice said, "Ma'am, may I help?" She lifted her head to see a man wearing an EMT badge kneel down beside her.

"Out back door," she panted. "Go!"

The man unclipped a radio from his waistband as he stood, and spoke rapid words into it. "Suspect exited the back door. Apprehend if possible." He raced out of the room. She heard his feet clatter down the stairs, then dash through the back of the house.

Her effort made the room spin, off balance, and she shut her eyes. "Ohhh." She gagged once and then squeezed her throat shut against the nausea.

A second set of engine sounds halted. A minute later, she heard Anders's voice speak her name. Then he had his arms beneath her. He lifted her up off the floor and placed her on Lisa's skewed bed.

Waves of pain made her squinch her eyelids tight shut. She groaned and then laid back. He pulled a pillow behind her head. He stroked her forehead.

"I'm here now, Marca. You're going to be okay."

She peeked through squinted eyes. *It really is him.*

Coughing for breath, she tried to speak, but no other sound came.

"What did he do to you?"

"Kicked." She forced it out. "EMT after him."

"What did he look like?"

"The drawing. Tall."

She heard footsteps again at the back door, and saw Anders's head swing around. His hand suddenly held his Glock.

"Stay still," he whispered, and cat-crept out the door, turning toward the stairs.

A long silence ensued before a voice from downstairs announced, "Emergency EMT. Are you the one who called for assistance?" Voices dropped to inaudible before three men returned upstairs.

"I'm sorry," the EMT said to Marca. "He planned his exit route well. We didn't even catch a glimpse of him, I'm afraid." He was back at her side, his partner standing just beyond him, nodding.

"Where did he kick you?" Anders asked, circling around the men until he stood by her head.

She pulled up her shirt on the right side. The kick had fallen just below her ribs. A patch of red and grey showed there, and the EMT moved in and probed it carefully. "Bruised," he said. "Do you hurt anywhere else?"

"My leg."

"A recent break?" The EMT asked as he examined her leg. "You better have it checked by a doctor in case the break shifted. We can transport you to the hospital."

"No," she said. "See my own doc."

"I'll make sure that happens," the detective said as he dismissed the EMT and his partner with a handshake. "You probably saved Marca's life by arriving before I could. Thank you for your help."

As the two men left, Marca let out the tears that had pressed against her eyelids for the past quarter-hour. "Anders, I was so afraid. It seemed like nobody would get here in time. He threatened to torture me. He might have killed me. I can't stop shaking. Sorry."

"Don't be sorry. It was my recommendation that you stay with a friend that put you into danger. I won't leave you alone again. I'm taking you by your doctor's office, and then moving you to my house. And I'll call a guard to stay with you while I'm at work. Can you walk? Let me get your crutches."

"Can we take my things?" She rose with help, catching her breath at the pain in her leg and side. She pressed her lips together and squinted her eyes as she attempted to shift her weight from the bed onto her crutches.

Gently, he took the crutches from her, laid them on the bed and lifted her into his arms. "You're in no shape to walk. I better carry you. Tell me where to find what you need when I come back, okay? Right now, I need to get you to the car."

Through the pain, Marca felt her body press against his warmth, supported in his arms. The pressure was a comfort that allowed her to let her tensed muscles relax. *I'm safe now.* She concentrated on the movement of his body and held on tight.

Chapter 20

While Marca received an examination from her doctor, Anders waited, trying to work out the details of having her stay at his place. *It isn't going to be easy.*

Anders pictured his condo—a blue-gray building about ten minutes drive from work. It was a single level, two-bedroom unit on the ground floor. The resident gardener kept the landscaping immaculate, with mixed rusts, greens and whites that formed a backdrop for the bursts of colorful petals in spring and summer.

Inside, Anders kept a tidy home, though utilitarian. Purchased prints, that he rarely noticed, hung on the walls. But the real chunk of his life on display was the set of framed and signed photos of each year's Little League team that lined the hallway, with Roy Tenison and he smiling beside the players they coached.

I'll make sure an armed guard stays with her whenever I am away at work. That was the easy part. He should have done it when she was at Lisa's.

But Marca needed a place to sleep. *Should I put her in the office?* He used his second bedroom as an office, and it held only a loveseat and his computer station with a wheeled chair pulled up to the desk. *At least she would have the privacy of a door that closed.* But no. There was no space for a person to stretch out on the loveseat. If anything, she needed more room than usual because of her injury, not less.

I'll just have to put her on the living room couch. But that was terribly public. And a real bed would be much better for her. She needed her own room. If he was honest, he needed that, too. A threshold he would cross only when necessary for her care.

I have to put her in my room. He gulped. What if he had to go inside to get something he needed? Could he possibly remember to move everything out of there—his clothes, shoes, work gear, ammunition and his gun, the items he carried in his pockets, Little League ball and glove—. He started a mental list.

He winced at the thought of what the police chief would say about the arrangement, but then he set his jaw. He wasn't going to back down. He wouldn't make the mistake of letting Marca's attacker find her alone again. When he had followed the department rules, it had been to her detriment. Now he would keep her close by, even though he might be out of order, or at the least, running the charred edges of acceptability.

Am I doing this because it's Marca? Anders felt a strong responsibility to protect the citizens of Woodsdale. He could honestly say he might make this decision in a similar situation for the protection of a victim who was being stalked—whose life was in danger.

But more is going on here. When he thought of Marca, a wave of protective affection swept through him that went beyond what he experienced toward others. He wanted her there for himself as well as for her protection. That meant he had to double-check his motivation constantly to be certain his behavior was appropriate. Prudent. Controlled.

No, it won't be easy. But he found himself looking forward to her stay. His heart beat faster.

* * *

Later, on the drive to his house, Marca said, "Anders, about our conversation last night—doesn't the person who kidnaps usually know his victim? It seems like somebody who knew Matthew, even though his alibi checked out, probably committed the crime."

"Quite possible."

"You said this guy was smart. Couldn't he have done that? Or maybe you've bypassed a group of people who seemed unlikely at first, like the potters. Are there people you didn't consider?"

"At the start, we did two things to get the case moving. We included as much crime scene data as we could, and we compared it to the groups of people most likely to contain the attacker. As we eliminate the most likely groups, we add new ones in. So I'll consider what groups we might have missed. If I come up with one, I'll thank you for the suggestion by taking you out for dinner when this is all over."

"It's a deal." She smiled at him before she continued.

"Did you find out whether Matthew had any enemies at the university—or ones his wife knew about? Professors bypassed for promotion? Past students? Old girlfriends? Jealous coworkers? That kind of thing?" she asked.

"Yes, but it's time to repeat those interviews."

"Since the crime occurred in a pottery lab, the guy probably has a connection to Matthew through ceramics."

"It would make sense, though nothing matched up from the college so far. I'll see whether they'll provide the names of students who received low grades from Matthew. They'll claim confidentiality issues in releasing that info, but he has good friends at the university who want the case solved."

"Get those with "C's" or below. A "C" can ruin a good GPA or get a major kicked out of some fields. I feel stupid saying all this. You obviously know it already," she said. She looked down at her hands and winced.

"I do, but I appreciate having my memory jogged. Thanks for reminding me to stay on top of the legwork." His smile was gentle.

* * *

Anders showed Tim's drawing to the woman who had taken in the cruiser at the detailer's. She had vines tattooed down her arms and wore a ring in her nose.

"Was this the man who brought in the car?" he asked.

"He wore a knitted cap, so I couldn't see his hair, but that face, uh, it just doesn't look right somehow—the shape, maybe. He was from the south, though. I heard it in his voice," she said.

Still, whether she remembered poorly, the suspect was disguised, or the drawing was inaccurate, the person who dropped off that car had to be either the kidnapper or an accomplice. He remembered wondering whether it had taken two men to carry Matthew from the pottery studio. This might be a second man involved in the abduction. And a southerner? That was new information.

On the other hand, the evidence people found nothing useful inside the detailed police cruiser, though they were just starting through the trash bags.

Nor was there any telltale residue on the tires. *But detailers are expert cleaners. Suspect seems smarter than most.*

* * *

Matthew hated to lose track of time.

I've missed two meal breaks, maybe more. Enemy didn't feed me dinner after the handoff, and probably missed breakfast as well.

He had been lulled by the regularity of Enemy's visits. He had used the commode before leaving for the handoff, but his need to urinate was growing constantly, not painful yet, but urgent. Still, he would have downed a bottle of water gratefully. His stomach gurgled at the thought.

When he first awakened, following the failed handoff, he suspected that he had missed his evening meal. He followed his routine and slept. Now, awakening again, he began his exercises as if breakfast had just passed. As far as he could gauge time, he suspected this was true. He tried to focus on the time of day and his schedule and away from the thought of breakfast. His stomach did more than growl when he thought about his hunger, it felt like it was trying to devour itself.

He had heard Enemy record the DVD for Alice before they went to the train station. The things Enemy said and the way he said them made him scowl, and he questioned whether the exchange would happen—the reason he had warned Alice to expect something irregular. He wasn't surprised to be returned to his box rather than released. He knew his getting free was a long shot. Finding himself deserted here was part of the suffering his captor intended. *He can't get to me. Won't let him inside my head.*

He had wiggled the pin out of the hinge last night, or nearly all the way out. He had pushed it back in before he could drop and lose it in the bottom of the box. He had worn through a part of the clasp that held it. But he needed food and water, so he didn't want his progress noticed, should Enemy return with breakfast. It seemed clear now that the kidnapper wasn't coming back again, at least not to feed him.

The link of his wrist chain was foil-thin as well. With a surface to press against, he knew that he could break it in a moment. That wouldn't remove the cuffs, but it would give him more freedom of motion.

It was time to give his breakout plan a try. He had to commit to the plan whole-heartedly, because once he pried and kicked the box's door, the damage would be apparent. He planned to tear the door from its remaining hinges.

I've exercised for a reason. I'm up for this.

He rejected any doubt that it was true.

Chapter 21

Anders strode to the vehicle pool office in quick steps. It was situated in a temporary building behind the Police Station. Because his own cruiser was assigned, he rarely visited the pool. But this was the second time today that he had come here. This time, he was seeking the information that could save a man's life.

He approached the receptionist.

"I'm trying to gather information about the car that was involved in the crime yesterday—the one I picked up the keys for earlier today. I'm the chief investigator on that case. I need to know how our suspect got those keys."

"The keys?" the receptionist said. "Those keys have hung here for weeks. The car hasn't been borrowed—at least not for awhile. But let me look in the safe. We keep a back-up set of keys for each car inside. I can see if those are missing."

"Thanks."

The receptionist came back quickly and shrugged. "The back-up keys are in the safe where they belong."

"Interesting. Tell me, is there any way a person could steal that vehicle without a key?"

"Even if an officer left the car door unlocked—and they are double-checked each night—our safety protocol causes the steering wheel to lock unless the correct key turns in the ignition. You can't steer a car you've hotwired," the receptionist said.

"That's what I thought. The suspect took the car in for detailing immediately following the crime, and told them he needed to bring back the keys so I could pick it up when they finished. They kept the car secure inside their garage since he left it unlocked for them. So he lied about needing to return the keys—distraction, I suppose, or the desire to keep the car hidden. He probably knew we'd have an APB out on it. He must have had his own set of keys, or borrowed them from another employee."

"That would make sense, except that pool vehicles are not assigned to people long term. They collect the keys with the vehicle and then turn them in together when they're done. Copying vehicle pool keys is forbidden—a quick way to join the unemployment line," the fellow said.

"I need a list of the individuals who borrowed that car this year. One of them duplicated keys, I'm positive. And by some means, our guy got ahold of them. I need to determine who it was."

"I'll need to okay that with my supervisor," the receptionist said, and jotted himself a note.

"Please do so now. The sooner I get that list, the better chance we'll save an innocent man's life."

The receptionist crumpled the note, his eyes widening. "Uh, I'll call right away, of course."

When the receptionist handed the list to Anders, he scanned it. Twelve people, including Ana, had borrowed the car, some on multiple dates.

He returned to his office, paper in hand, and placed it in the center of his desk. Then he dialed Marca. He studied the kids in the group photo of this year's Little League team as he waited for her to answer.

"Are you comfortable over there? Do you feel safe?" he asked, setting the photo aside when he heard her voice.

"Better all the time, though now and then I flash on how I felt when the kidnapper grabbed me. Somehow, after going through yesterday's scare, instead of thinking I'm going to break down, I'm getting stronger inside—better able to handle the stress. And the guard you have over here is awesome. I told him my concerns. He's a good listener."

"Glad to hear. Hey, I owe you a big thank you for suggesting that I open the investigation to new groups of people."

"How's that?"

"Our suspect knew a cop with keys to that police car—someone who made an illicit set. You opened my eyes to investigating my own department's officers. If this pans out, let's celebrate. I'll pay up and buy us dinner, okay?"

"I'd never turn down that opportunity, Anders."

"Good. I've got calls to make, but I'll catch you up this evening."

* * *

A few minutes later, Jessica St. Marie darted in with Alice's cellphone on speaker, and sat next to Anders. The suspect was on the phone again.

"You involved the police against my orders," the alien voice accused.

"I did not go to the police. Please believe me. There was a mix-up."

"You did. When your husband handed me your backpack, the man nearest him on the sidewalk was an out-of-uniform cop I've seen dozens of times. I looked straight into his eyes. There was no mistake, so quit lying to me." His voice rose in volume.

"Maybe he was just that—an off-duty cop who happened to walk along the street just then. They don't work 24/7. I didn't ask him or any police to take part in the handoff. I played it just the way you asked."

"I'm not stupid. Either you or that Ruiz lady got the cops involved against my orders. I'm finished with both of you, and I'm done with your husband. He can rot for all I care. As I promised, he is suffering now. You figure out how to find him before he starves to death. I withdraw my aid."

"You got your money."

"That's the only reason he isn't dead. You bought his life. Now you rescue him while it lasts!" In a snap, he was gone, off the line.

"I think our time just ran out. Is that team that was searching out old houses with root cellars knocking doors yet?" Anders asked Jessica.

"I'll check immediately."

While he waited, Anders called the P.D. employees who had driven the now-detailed cruiser during the past year, except Ana. He started with the most recent on his list and worked backwards, leaving messages for most people. The two he caught live were adamant that they had never duplicated keys for any squad car, and one quoted him regulations on the subject. *Well, someone is going to hear this message and feel my breath on the back of his neck. I'm coming closer, suspect man.*

Next, he called Ana about the results of the trace evidence from the SUV.

"Anything yet, sweet stuff?"

"Hey blondie. Results just back—let me look. Yes, one hair bagged from the pottery studio matches one found in the SUV. Other hair didn't match, so was probably from later renters of the vehicle."

"Run all the evidence against our department's personnel files, will you? I suspect he's a city employee, and possibly a cop."

"Absolutely. We had a latent off the kiln door that matched the DNA in that hair sample. Could be your suspect. Of course, we found a number of prints and hairs that matched, but most were people who used the studio regularly. The unidentified prints shouldn't take long to run. We've all been printed."

"Thanks. By the way, when you've driven a vehicle from the pool, did you ever make duplicate keys?"

"No way. Wouldn't want the responsibility of keeping them safe. Not to mention, it's not cool with the department."

He explained about the keys. "We're closing in on this guy, but time is not our friend. If you isolate hair from the detailed cruiser out of that trash you brought back, I expect you'll find another match to this guy. I'd sure like to know who he is."

"For you, I'll expedite it," she said.

He knew she would.

He set down the phone and chewed the inside of his cheek. *I'm on your heels, you bastard. Who the hell are you?*

In that moment, a realization flooded over him. He gasped out loud. *The drawing. Of course, the drawing!* He drew it out from under a pile of evidence reports, and examined it with fresh eyes. Although it had not resembled anyone he knew when he studied it before, he now recognized the suspect's face in an instant. A shudder passed through him, yet he could not bring himself to believe what he saw without verification. He grabbed the team photo from his desk and stared at it in silence.

His heart thudded. *Oh my God. Roy.* There was no question. It was his co-coach of the Little League team. Officer Roy Tenison.

Chapter 22

He played the suspect's video again, studying the man. *Yes, that could be Roy under the mask.* He ran his finger down the list of those who had borrowed the cruiser. Roy's name leaped out at him.

Bits of evidence fell together like jigsaw puzzle pieces. *Did I blind myself because we coach together?* Tenison could easily have done it all: made the keys, watched Marca pick up Alice's cellphone, listened under Marca's window during the potluck, disguised his voice, found out where Marca had been moved from the officers in his group without drawing suspicion to himself. *So bold.* The only thing missing was a motive.

Anders darted down the hall to Roy's office. The door was locked. *Where is that bastard? He was at work this morning.*

Back in his office, he called Roy's home number, but got no answer. He left a message about Little League that he hoped sounded innocuous and then hung up.

Then he called the chief with the news.

"Tenison? One of our officers is the kidnapper? Damn it all!" Anders heard the thud of a fist hitting the desk, and the crash of something falling. The chief's language degraded as he railed at the betrayal. Anders grimaced as the phone's volume pegged. "I want to twist that maggot's head off and watch his eyes pop out. He's going to wish . . . ," the chief ranted on for several minutes.

When he finally slowed down, the chief agreed to fund any plan necessary to carve this tumor from the body of his department. He became generous. Finally, Anders received the go-ahead for the extra staff he needed.

After he hung up, Anders called for a search warrant on Roy's residence, summarizing the facts that pointed to the officer. The judge was clearly intrigued, and offered to send over his student intern to pick up the evidence for his review. That seemed hopeful.

Then Anders compiled multiple packets of copied photos: two of Matthew, Roy Tenison's police pic, the cruiser and the black SUV, and an enlargement from the video, showing Roy in his mask with the rough wall of the cellar behind him. These they would show to local residents as they canvassed.

While he waited for the officers to arrive, he called Alice with the update.

"I will take part in the search for Matthew," Alice said, in her no-questions voice. "You can't stop me unless you lock me up, so you might as well tell me what's going on."

Anders didn't try to dissuade her. After the failed handoff, he doubted anyone could. "Get over here right away then. You will work as part of a two-person team, and follow identical procedures to the rest of us. If your partner is concerned about your ability to do the work, you're off the team. We head out immediately after the briefing."

He looked up at the picture of Matthew that he had taped up in his office. Matthew looked down at him from next to the clock, which seemed to tick away the final moments of his life. No time left to rest, no time to eat, no time to think about Marca, who could be "the one," no time to do anything but find the bad guy and bring Matthew Fyre home alive. *How long can you wait, Matt, old man? Hold on, I'm coming for you.*

The officers gathered, stunned at the news that Roy was involved. They became convinced that Anders was correct about his identity after a short swing through the evidence. When Anders passed around the drawing, everyone muttered. Heads shook in disbelief. Curses sounded. He realized he wasn't the only person who had blinded himself to the possibility of a perpetrator from inside the P.D.

"We need to find him—and fast." Anders spoke to the group. "The only task that is more time sensitive is finding Matthew, whose life is at risk. Possibly where one is, we'll find the other, unless Roy is at home. He's been too smart so far for me to imagine he'd imprison Matthew there, where we might surprise him with a warrant.

"He probably suspects that we'll zero in on him, now that the detailed cruiser is back in our possession. Before I realized he was our man, I left a message asking if he had made keys to the stolen cruiser. He knows we're at least getting close to identifying him.

"Please don't discuss the search outside of this group. There's a chance he may not have acted alone. We don't know if another officer is involved—no forensic evidence points to one. But Alice Fyre was correct to hold back information within the department earlier in this investigation." He nodded at her and she nodded back. "Let's not get sloppy now. He could rabbit before we can seize him. Don't let him know we're coming—no lights or sirens near his house."

"Could he still be in this building?" the senior officer asked. "I saw him here this morning."

"It's possible."

"Then, I'll search it," the officer said, "before I join you all at the canvassing site."

"Excellent. Someone else can stake out his home."

"I'll cover Roy's place," Benjamin said, in a grim tone.

"If you see evidence that he is at home, or if you see him enter, call for backup immediately. We won't be far away. I expect to get a search warrant, but I don't want to disturb the house before he gets there. Too much opportunity for a tip off by some sign of our presence. I'd like to have the house surrounded, with him inside, before we go in. And we need to do it as a group. No solo heroics."

"Understood."

"I need every remaining body for the house-to-house search. We'll look for root cellars in the older neighborhoods. I'll be with you, and so will Matthew's wife, Alice. We'll join the team, headed by Peter, that has been on task since last night.

"Only enter a house with the permission of the resident. I expect that many may offer to help by showing us their cellars. See how closely any exposed dirt wall matches the pic from the video. Keep track of those you find most probable—photograph them if possible, and note the addresses.

"If the citizens recognize Roy, Matthew or either car, let me know immediately. Good luck everyone."

He directed several pairs to join yesterday's crew, and the others to canvass a second neighborhood of older homes. A sense of purpose grew nearly palpable as the officers and Alice left the room.

* * *

At 10:00 p.m., Anders reluctantly asked his teams to stop for the night. Roy hadn't been found in the police department. No activity was evident at his house, though lights were on, and Benjamin was watching.

The photos were unfamiliar to the canvassed residents. But there had been successes—several cellars were photographed in each neighborhood.

"Excellent work. Thank you for your dedication. Let's start the hunt again at 8:00 tomorrow morning. Check messages before then, and I'll tell you where to meet. Sleep well, everyone. Tomorrow we get our man."

Anders would have willingly continued throughout the night, but he expected spotty responses to police knocks and anger from people interrupted after they'd retired. The police needed maximum cooperation from residents. The more pushback they encountered, the less progress they could expect to make, regardless of their efforts. *Hold on, Fyre. You can make it.* He hoped it. He prayed it.

Ana had arranged for a staff member to remain at work all night with her, if necessary, analyzing photos of cellars and soil from the walls of basements that remained unfinished. She expected, before morning, to know exactly where the teams should concentrate their search. She promised that the information would await Anders on his phone when he came in.

The stakeout at Roy's house would continue through the night. Anders asked for a call at any sign of activity within, or if the suspect entered or left the house. He promised to keep his cellphone turned on, right beside his bed.

* * *

Matthew could hold it no longer. He urinated into his pants, and woke from a toilet dream, cursing. His urine had become concentrated, and it burned where his skin wore thin from the exercises. He put the smell out of his mind, and focused on actions that remained under his control.

I've missed another meal. I'm on my own.

Earlier, he had formulated a plan. Now, he took action. He pulled the pin out of the damaged hinge, and pushed it with one thumb just over the top and into his front pants pocket—at least, he believed he had gotten it inside, despite his restricted mobility. *No matter. I doubt I'll need it again.*

He hammered and kicked the door above him. It rattled each time. *Not a lot of leverage for my kicks.* He had only inches between his foot and the cabinet door. As he had done with the hinge, he did with the door—made up for minimal progress by repeating his actions.

Reveling in his leg cramps, which highlighted the extent of his efforts, he continued to assault the coffin box. When he could kick no longer, he twisted the rubber toe of his shoe into the narrow crack between the door and the box and pried, attempting to enlarge the opening. More shoe wedged through, and he grinned as he panted. *I'm making progress.* When that foot tired, he switched to the one on the padlocked side and pried again. *No telling which will yield first.*

As both feet tired, he devised a new tactic, wiggling his body down as far toward the base of the box as he could manage. Then with feet flat against the baseboard, and his arms jammed against the sides of the box with all their strength, he thrust hard against the board, capitalizing on the slight bend the box allowed in his knees. The large muscles of his legs bulged, then won out over his smaller arm muscles, and his body slid away from the base. He repeated the sequence over and over again, knowing the board had to give way in time. Then he began the series of escape moves all over again, trading out exercises for those most vital to his survival.

After several cycles, Matthew thought he perceived a slight spring in the footboard, which gave him a renewed burst of power. His activity distracted him from his wet pants, his growling stomach and his dry mouth. His mood was improving as well. *I like hitting back. At last!*

* * *

Anders let himself into his apartment as quietly as possible. He didn't want to waken Marca. It was after midnight.

The guard, in the small office at the opposite side of the hall, stood as Anders entered, and they spoke softly together. He sent the man home for a nap before he needed to return at 5:45 a.m., when Anders left for work again.

It seemed, from the guard's report, that Marca had retired early—a couple of hours ago. Anders was glad she was resting. She'd been through so much, and a lot of it was his fault. He shook his head. *I'll make up for it once the case closes.*

Anders wondered if he would be able to sleep at all. His body was coiled for action like a cobra about to strike. He'd wanted to find Matthew in the search tonight, and was irritated by the lack of resolution. He would have kept canvassing if he could have done so responsibly.

In the kitchen, he opened the refrigerator and stood gazing inside while seeing only the scenes of the day behind his eyes. He shivered as the cold air chilled him. At last he reached for a half-empty bottle of wine. *Maybe this'll help me unwind.*

"Anders, is that you?" a soft voice called from the bedroom.

He walked to the doorway with the bottle in hand. "Sorry I woke you. I thought I could use a glass of wine before bed."

"May I join you?" Marca asked.

She had propped the top half of her body up on pillows. Anders recognized the skimpy black nightshirt that he had packed up with her things from Lisa's place. He couldn't help imagining her in the thin fabric when he first saw it, but the reality made him catch his breath. The light from the hall accentuated the contours of her breasts beneath the thin material. He thought he could even make out the shape of her nipples.

She had the sheet pulled up over her good leg. But the injured leg, elevated, had caused the nightgown to slide back and expose the dark satin skin of her upper thigh.

Anders swallowed. "Sure," he said. "I'll be right back." He returned to the kitchen, breathing deeply, unable to get this vision of Marca out of his mind. He poured two glasses of wine and returned to the bedroom.

He pulled a chair up by the head of the bed, carefully setting it where he could admire the view, but couldn't reach Marca without effort. They sipped the rich red liquid, speaking a few words about the day just past, and then fell into an electric silence. He felt giddy—the wine, he supposed.

Moving Marca to his house for her protection now seemed like a perilous venture. He shivered in an unexpected flood of tingles at the thought. So he concentrated on finishing his wine, swirling it in the glass and watching it closely between sips.

When Anders stood to retire, still glowing from the wine, he saw Marca lick her lips. He imagined kissing her. Her mouth looked so enticing. Her smile made him think that she also wanted him to cross that line with her.

Instead, he wished her goodnight, took the glasses to the kitchen, and washed them thoroughly. As he worked, he shook his head, no longer sure whether he had made the right decision bringing her here. *It shouldn't be for long. We could get this guy tomorrow.* As much as he liked the thought of capturing the suspect, he wasn't sure he wanted a reason for Marca to leave.

His lip twisted in a wry smile, and he imagined his logic and his feelings as little minion warriors in an animated battle.

I won't need work to keep me awake tonight — not with Marca in the next room.

Chapter 23

When he got home, Roy checked the messages on his work phone, and found that Johanson was calling officers about the stolen cruiser. *So. It is time to pack up.*

He peeked under a corner of an upstairs curtain and searched the street. *No unusual cars.* Still, he'd be careful.

Always, he kept his curtains closed, but he turned on all the lights he'd need now, before it got dark. In case anyone was watching him, he made sure never to cross between a light and a window, where his shadow would show. He'd let them guess whether someone was at home or not.

Cushioning his laptop into its original packing, he slipped that into the cardboard carton where his printer had gone a few minutes before. Those were two of the things he knew he'd need. Wherever he went. *Goodbye Woodsdale P.D.*

One great thing about being a cop these past six years had been gathering information on illegal activities. He had learned how to obtain false identity records for his new start: passport, driver's license, birth certificate, and diplomas. From his desk, he picked up the coded list of contact information for those who created personal documents and tucked it into his wallet. He put all his other papers through the shredder. It whirred, and tiny scraps of paper filled its discard bin. *Adios, old life.*

Yes, being a cop had been a good job, one that he wouldn't have left except for the chance to get revenge on Fyre for ruining his love life. He got steamed when he remembered it. His fiancé left him while taking Fyre's classes. She got so involved in ceramics that she didn't have time to make him dinner, let alone attend to his other needs.

All she talked about was Fyre—like he was some kind of god. It was like she traded personalities with some uppity loser with a chip on her shoulder. His obedient little woman, the one who worshiped the ground he walked upon, vanished. She looked the same, but she wouldn't even wear that crotchless panty set he bought her for her birthday. Said "it felt degrading." *The bitch.*

If it weren't for Fyre, they'd still have the perfect relationship. Prior to the ceramics class she belonged to Roy in every way—looked at him with that expression she later gave Fyre. He knew he'd still have her except for their constant arguments about her taking Fyre's classes. So getting back at Fyre was too great an opportunity to miss. *Suffer, you bastard, suffer good.*

The ransom money was an unanticipated bonus. For years in the future he'd have no need to work again. *Plenty of time to develop a new identity elsewhere.* He smiled.

He tossed his cordless mouse and its pad into the computer box along with his few CDs and memory sticks. Then he thought of the ceramicist locked in the basement of the old house. That flipped his smile into a scowl. He was supposed to be done with the man. But Fyre had become a complication—a loose end that needed tying up.

If he killed the guy, the whole force would come after him. In such numbers, they might get lucky and catch him. At the same time, however, the police were proving too inept to reach the ceramicist before he died of thirst. *How lame. Now I have to decide whether or not to give Fyre water before I leave.*

He thought of Johanson and the other police. He snorted. *Idiots.* As they realized who'd taken Fyre, they'd have to appreciate the beauty of his crime. He chuckled to himself. *A great way to retire.* And it was about the right time. He needed to work with people who were closer to his intellectual level. Maybe in a larger city he'd find more gifted people who appreciated his brilliance. He enjoyed being recognized—looked up to—like by the kids on the Little League team. But they were only kids.

He didn't worry much about Fyre himself. After all, he deserved to suffer. In his imagination, he liked seeing Fyre at the edge of death by the time the cops released him, needing a long rehabilitation in one of those degrading nursing homes filled with mindless hulks of useless flesh. But he wanted his recent cohorts to find the man alive—just on the verge of breathing his last.

He knew that the department would do their best to come after a killer, even across state lines. With no wrongful death, however, they'd give up on the case fairly quickly, and shift it to the unsolved file. He knew how the politics worked. Only the most recent and newsworthy crimes got attention. *Not enough money to track down everyone.*

He carried the computer box out to his car in the garage. It sat with doors and trunk open to minimize the sound of opening and closing. He smiled, smug at the thought of how he kept ahead of his pursuers.

Too bad about the furnishings he had purchased. He'd select just a few favorite things, maybe a
box worth, to make his new place, wherever it was,
feel homey. After six years he'd gathered quite a bit.
Looking around the garage, he grabbed an appropri-
ate-sized box to take upstairs.

He wandered from room to room, picking up a
handful of items. It surprised him how ordinary they
all looked. *Just stuff. Time to move on.*

He remembered a childhood scrapbook, and
carried it to the car with his half-filled box, then went
back for his suitcases and some electronics in boxes.
The rest can stay. I have money. I can start again.

He quietly closed up his car, bumping the doors
with one hip to latch them securely. *If I have to leave
quickly, everything is packed. Now I can get some sleep.*
He'd decide about Fyre in the morning. Should he get
water for the old fart, or let him thirst?

* * *

Anders arrived in the office a little before 6:00
a.m. The search warrant for Roy's residence was in
his box. He checked out the photos and listened to
Ana's summary of the night's work.

"The initial neighborhood had a soil composition most similar to the one in the kidnapper's video,"
her voice said on his machine. "Concentrate your
search there. Good luck, blue eyes."

That's my girl.

He left a message for his officers. Those who had
started there would continue where they left off. Referring to a map of the area, he left addresses for his
transferred group where they should begin their
morning. They'd work neighboring streets, so that
everybody would be nearby if needed.

He was still about a half-hour away from reporting to the location. He didn't want to awaken the res-

idents too early. Glancing at the clock, he thought of one more action he could take to further the investigation—search Roy's office.

It was P.D. property. Last night when he talked to the chief, he not only received permission to check Roy's office, but the chief offered to drop by with a key. That was also in his box.

He called Ana and caught her in, despite her late night. *I bet she spent the night here. Amazing woman.* He explained what he was about to do. She promised to follow him over with disposables.

Before she hung up she said, "You know, I can't help feeling a kind of self-righteous satisfaction that Roy is our kidnapper."

"You two didn't get along?"

She snorted. "I tried to be friendly when he first arrived—to help him feel part of the team. But he took my teasing all wrong. Before I knew it, he had me trapped in a storage closet, pressing his body up against me as if he expected I'd drop my pants for him. Like he was worth risking my job over." She rolled her eyes.

"You never told me that."

"Well, it was awkward, Anders. Sheesh."

"So what happened?"

"I gave him a knee to the groin—not enough to lay him up, but enough that he knew he was out of line. After that, I was careful to keep from meeting one-on-one with him. Over the years, I've relaxed about it, since he never came on to me again. But of all the cops in the department, Roy is one I don't mind bringing down."

* * *

Anders unlocked Roy's office and opened the door, letting Ana precede him inside. Little in the office expressed the personality of its assigned occupant. Few personal expressions graced the place—no family photos, news clippings on the corkboard, plants, or indications of avocations Roy enjoyed. Not even a reference to the Little League coaching he shared with Anders.

Grabbing a pen from his pocket, Anders pulled open the center desk drawer. It contained only the expected: pencils, pens, erasers, paperclips, scissors, and sticky notepads. He shut it, still using the pen, and opened a side drawer the same way. Inside it rested Roy's calendar book. Anders caught his breath. Careful not to mar possible fingerprints, he lifted its cover with his pen and tried to get a peek inside.

"Ana, Look—here is Roy's calendar. I need a look at it. Can you get prints and whatever else you need from it, rush-rush? It might contain info to help us direct today's search for Matthew."

"Tell you what, detective man. We can share. I'll photograph each page. Then you get the pics and I keep the book."

"Good enough, darling," he said. "Can you send copies to my cellphone as soon as they're ready? I'll be out in the field."

"I'll shoot you the photos, blue eyes. And soon. But I need to photograph the drawer before I can remove the calendar. "

"Thanks Ana. It's a life or death kind of day."

"May you find him alive. I'll keep my eyes open for anything else that might help as I finish going through Roy's office."

"Thanks. I have to run now. We have houses to search. Questions to ask. A kidnapper to throw behind bars for a long stay."

She smiled and nodded. "Do it, babe. I'll be cheering you on." She turned back to photograph the drawer with the calendar.

Chapter 24

Anders knocked on a door.

"Good morning ma'am. I'm Detective Johanson, Woodsdale Police. We are investigating a crime that we believe occurred in this area. I wondered if you could answer some questions to help us." He held out his ID for her examination.

"Sure, I suppose," she said, not opening the door any farther.

He slipped her the photos of Matthew and Roy through the gap. "Would you look at these people and tell me if you've seen them in the area?"

"I don't think so."

"How about these cars, ma'am. Do they look familiar?"

"Can't say I've seen them, but I'm not a car aficionado, I'm afraid."

"Is there a cellar in your house, ma'am?"

"A cellar? Yes. Why do you ask?"

"This crime was a kidnapping. The man who was kidnapped is being held in a cellar—one with unfinished walls—like in an old fashioned root cellar. Does that sound similar to yours, ma'am?"

"Oh no. We finished ours. Most of the neighbors did, too. But all these older homes started out with unfinished basements."

"Could we see how you finished yours, please?"

The woman looked at him and away several times, shuffling her feet, but then said, "Okay. I guess there's no harm in that, if it will help find the kidnapper." She opened the door wider and he saw she was wearing a bathrobe.

He and Peter, his partner for the day, followed her down a long stairway. The cellar, framed in wood, had been dry-walled, and painted. He observed spots where flat nail heads changed the texture of the drywall. A dated, semi-professional job.

"Oh yes, I see. Thank you," Anders said. "Do any houses in the neighborhood still have unfinished cellars?"

"I don't think so. I haven't seen an unfinished cellar in years."

"How about pointing out some houses where you don't know whether the cellars are finished?"

From her front door, she indicated houses she was unsure of. Anders marked them on a map, and Peter jotted down her name and house number. As the officers stepped off the front stoop to the sidewalk Anders said, "We need to move forward with this search as quickly as we can in order to find Matthew alive. If we mark whether houses are reported as finished, unfinished, or unknown, we can hit the more likely houses first and visit the finished ones later if necessary."

"Good time saver," Peter said, nodding, and they targeted the nearest house that the woman had no information about. As they walked, Anders composed a group text to the other teams to share his idea.

Putting away his cell, he indicated the house's steps with a sideways flick of his hand. "Your turn to go first." Peter led onto the porch and rang the bell. *This could take awhile.*

* * *

Matthew awoke, not remembering when he slid into sleep. *I'm weaker.*

His mind played games with him; dreams swirled into waking leaving him unsure what was real. He kept his eyes closed to the darkness, which otherwise made him strain to see, even when he coached himself not to. He saw *things* that must be hallucinations. Closed eyes were his best defense against them.

He kicked the top of the box, and held it up one-footed while he felt along the bottom edge with the other. The crack had expanded, and he estimated, through his athletic shoes, that it measured an inch in width this time. It opened widest at the corner; then it narrowed up the left side as far as he managed to shove his fingers toward the next intact hinge. *Surely it's loosening by now.*

He rested a moment before jamming his left shoe into the corner. He twisted and wiggled his foot until the toe pushed through. He pulled it back. Hope flared. He repeated the maneuver. Once the door lifted, he forced his right shoe under the door as well. His feet remained there, toes stuck under the door, as he rested. Cooler air flowed through the opening and tickled his nostrils. He inhaled a deep breath of hope.

Weakness came mainly from lack of water. His head ached, and his thoughts grew slower—both signs of dehydration. As long as he rested between assaults on the box, breaking free still seemed possible.

Bending his left elbow, he swept his forearm in an arc until his hand pointed toward his head. Reaching with his left hand, he searched along the join for another hinge, but couldn't reach one. He swiveled his hand back toward his feet and tried inching his fingers up the crack to where it narrowed. He bet the hinge was located near his waist, between the two extremes of his reach.

He wiggled his left foot and moved his shoe up the crack toward the hinge until his knee hit the door. He scooted his body toward the top end of the box and moved his wedged shoe farther up the left side. Scooting again, he bent his head hard over to the side until his neck protested, and repeated the movement. The shoe stuck there, and he knew pressure on the hinge was greater. Scooting once more, he jerked the shoe upward once more, yelling a Karate *Keyi* as he did so, then twisted his foot out of the shoe and left it behind. He slid back down flat in the box, panting.

With his left hand, he grasped the shoe. He twisted it, levering the door up as far as he could, released it, and twisted again with a grunt. Until his arm muscles fatigued too much to continue, he manipulated the shoe to widen the opening, alternately moving it closer toward the hinge.

Then, driving his toes against the door of the box, he swore at the thing, letting his anger fuel his strength. His efforts made no noticeable change, but afterward he found it easier to be patient—even lying thirsty in the darkness. He distracted himself from his discomfort while active, and the crazy thoughts backed away for a time. It was probably illusion, but the cool air coming through the crack seemed to fill his lungs more fully, too.

* * *

Ana photographed the pages of Roy's calendar book and sent a copy to Anders. She also forwarded them to a cryptologist for analysis. She hoped one or the other would discern a clue that would speed up the quest to find Matthew. In the back of the calendar, slid into its plastic cover, she found a key. *A padlock key.* She dusted it for prints, lifted what she could, then dialed Anders.

"Hey big man. I found a key in Roy's office. Shall I bring it to you?"

"I'll take any help love, short or long shots."

"Give me your location. I'd enjoy a little fresh air and your handsome face."

Anders read out the address of the house they would visit next. "Continue east down the street from there. If we're inside a house, just wait. We'll come out again soon."

"Great. I'll find you. Oh, the photos are on your phone right now. Haven't had a chance to examine them closely, but forwarded them to a woman who is a whiz when it comes to breaking code."

As he ended the call, a ring came from Benjamin who was watching Roy's house. "I think I saw some movement—he's in there. This may be our best chance to surround the house and nab him."

Anders phoned the case officers, directed them to Roy's and told them to surround the house. "Stay quiet and keep yourselves and your cars out of sight. If unaware, he may fall right into our trap. I have the warrant. We'll go for him as soon as we're all in place." It irritated him that he couldn't use his radio—made for situations like this, where multiple people needed information at once. But Roy had his own and might hear the call.

Leaving Alice with the remaining officers to canvass houses, they ran for their cruisers. Anders wove in, out, and around cars that responded too gradually to his flashing red and blues, which he left on until a few blocks from Roy's house.

He was the first at the site. Parking around the corner from the suspect's house, he drew his gun and crept up the street, ducking behind any shelter that might mask him. He looked up abruptly as a car backed out of Roy's driveway. An unmarked car, parked a block up the street, pulled out and followed.

"Crap. Too late," Anders said aloud, though nobody was nearby to hear him. He speed-dialed Benjamin as he ran back to his cruiser.

"I arrived as he left. Glad you were following. Any idea where he's off to?"

"Negative. I'll stay on his tail. Head back to the canvassing area. If he's decided to visit Matthew, you'll be nearer to him from there. I'll call if he turns off in a different direction," Benjamin said.

Ana was waiting patiently with the key when Anders returned with the other officers. His cell vibrated against his hip.

"Stay inside your car and keep the engine purring," Benjamin said. I'll have a house number for you in a moment. I'm on Lincoln Street now."

Anders restarted his car. "I'll keep this line open," he said to Benjamin. He waved out the window at Ana. "Benjamin promised me an address where Matthew may be stashed. Can you let the others know? I want to keep my line to him open."

"Sure thing, babe," Ana said. She took her cellphone from her pocket and called the officers he named. "Hey, it's been awhile since I got to see some action. May I hitch along?"

"You armed?"

"You betcha."

At that moment Benjamin spoke to Anders. "He stopped at a house on Taft, off of Lincoln. 7425. Closed the garage behind his car. I was a couple blocks behind, so I turned left just before I got to his house and parked at the corner, facing out for a quick follow, if necessary. Let me know if you want me there on foot, or here on watch."

"I'm on my way," Anders said. "Let's use your car as our meeting point."

"Roger."

He beckoned, Ana jumped into his car, and they zoomed off.

Chapter 25

Roy entered the rental house through the garage, climbed the stairs up to the main floor, and then opened the door at the top of a second set of stairs that descended to the cellar. He made little noise, but Fyre was usually awake and waiting for him.

This time, he heard knocking, groaning and cursing from the box where Dr. Fyre was imprisoned. He snuck down the stairs to see what the prisoner was up to. Fyre had shoved the door of the box up about four inches. It was held up by what? *An athletic shoe.* He almost laughed out loud. The door to the box was warped by Fyre's efforts.

Roy walked over to the wall and flicked on the light. The box went quiet. Then, he grabbed a loose water bottle from the case near the stairs. He walked to the box, and in one movement, twisted open the bottle and let it pour onto the lid. It cascaded past the opening Fyre had made. Roy laughed.

"Here's today's water." He watched the hand come out of the opening, trying to cup some of the water before it all dripped away. He imagined the agonizing trip it would have to reach Fyre's lips in the narrow space and laughed again. *He won't get more than a few drops.* He tossed the empty bottle at the box before heading back up the steps. He turned off the light at the top of the stairs and re-locked the door. *This stiff'll last awhile yet. Forget him.* Everything was happening as planned.

* * *

Anders pulled up next to Benjamin's car and conferred with him through the window before parking further down the side road. In a space beside an eight-foot high hedge, he pulled behind a local car that shielded his cruiser from the main road. He and Ana jogged back to join Benjamin.

Another car arrived, and Anders directed the cop to cover the near side of the house. Next Alice turned up, uninvited. Peter Landsbury and the senior officer pulled up behind her and got out.

"Oh no. You can't be here," Anders told Alice, climbing out of his car. "It's not allowed."

"I'm not leaving. You'll have to arrest me," she said, her chin in the air.

Anders looked around at the officers. "Good idea. I'll detain you." He opened the back door to his car. "Into the back seat, Alice. Don't make me hand-cuff you."

Alice's mouth fell open. "You're kidding, right? You can't keep me away from my husband."

At Anders' glance, the others circled closer to her.

"Not kidding, sorry. I let you partner with an-other officer to canvass door to door, but I cannot have you at the scene of the arrest. This is a police ac-tion," he told her, a no-nonsense look on his face. "If you are threatened, you will divert an officer to pro-tect you. Then we may lose Roy or Roy may kill Matthew so he can't testify. Get in the car. I'll come for you when it's safe again. Do you understand?"

She looked like she was about to argue, but the senior officer said, "You don't have a choice about climbing into that cruiser, ma'am. Your only choice is whether you get in by yourself or whether we assist you."

She climbed into the car, muttering expletives under her breath. The door swung shut. There was no door handle on the inside. "Hey. Don't forget me out here," she said, her eyes widening.

"I won't," Anders said.

He sent Peter to the back of the house with Ana, and directed the other officer to cover the far side of the house.

"Stay out of sight of the windows, everyone. Set your cellphones on vibrate so they won't be heard. Keep radio silence; he could be listening. Let's go."

They spread out, Anders and Benjamin at the front of the house. Anders studied the main door from a distance. *Sturdy — not amenable to opening with the flashy kick of a TV cop.* And they weren't TV cops.

"I'll try the knob; you check the windows," he said.

He slipped up the concrete stairs and eased his ear flat against the door. Eyes closed, he listened for a full minute. *Nothing.* He grasped the knob in both hands, one steadying while the other twisted it clockwise. When the handle turned no farther, he pulled, gradually increasing his strength until he was certain the door wouldn't open. *Locked.* With care, he untwisted the knob and listened once more for movement inside. Confident that his effort had gone unnoticed, he rejoined his partner and shook his head no.

Benjamin led him to a picture window, curtained and within easy reach. One side of it displayed louvered slats, also locked. Anders nodded and gave Benjamin thumbs up.

Then he backed away from the house and called his officers. He asked about possible escape routes they could see. Windows on the far side of the house were reported as high up, though lower ones were visible on the near side. Still, the back door sounded like the most plausible escape route that the suspect might attempt.

"I heard a cry from inside. Very faint," Peter said into his cell.

"Check your sightlines, and if it is safe, listen at the back door," Anders told him.

He listened to a rustle and soft steps. Then, several minutes passed.

"Nothing," Peter said in a soft voice.

"Keep your ears open. Let me know what happens," he said. I'll call again as soon as we have our plan of attack worked out." He hung up his cellphone.

* * *

Is there anything here to take along? Roy ran through the items in the house in memory, but came up with nothing. Other than groceries, he stored little in this recent rental. Only Fyre. He kept curtains drawn and the house locked up. Most rooms remained unfurnished, and he had avoided meeting any of his neighbors.

In the kitchen, he prepared food for the road, using up his sandwich makings. *I won't have to stop until I need gas.* As he spread the mayonnaise, a loud yell sounded from the cellar. He smiled, imagining the battle against the box. *Enjoy yourself, Fyre.*

* * *

Outside, Peter also heard the shout. He jerked a finger at the house, and raised his eyebrows at Ana. She nodded yes—she had caught it, too. He dialed Anders.

"We heard something again. A yell, from inside. It was faint out here, but I could discern effort behind it. Could be Matthew," Peter said.

"That helps our case. I'm sure we're legally covered. Exigent circumstances will stand up in court on this, both because he is poised to get away via car, and because you heard someone call out.

"Next task is to get inside. The front door is a no-go unless we trick him into opening it. A front window sounds like more dependable access," Anders said.

"The window's chosen. No problem," Benjamin said.

"Okay Peter, Ana," he said into the phone. "We're going in the front. We'll move fast," Anders said.

"Can one of us pull a car across the driveway to block that exit as well?" Ana asked.

"Excellent idea. Come get my keys and do it. I'll send the officer from the far side of the house to the back as soon as I hang up. Alert the fellow on the near side of what's about to go down on your way over to me." He hung up the phone and turned to Benjamin.

"I'll ring the bell at the front door. You cut through the window while I distract the suspect. Make as little noise as possible. I'll keep the radio on at my end, but only so you can hear what happens inside. If you speak, he may hear you. Use cellphones for other communications.

"Nobody enter until Benjamin and I pin down the suspect unless you hear otherwise. Then you're all invited to the party. We'll want to check the house for an accomplice or booby traps. Got it?" He quickly filled in the other officer.

"Let's move."

* * *

Roy pushed his sandwich into a zipped bag as the doorbell rang. He froze. *Who is that?* He tiptoed to the front door. It had no peephole. *Imagine that. Crappy old house.*

He considered moving straight for his car, but curiosity slowed him. *A Jehovah's Witness? A neighbor with a welcome casserole?* He sneered at the door. *Losers. What do you losers know about real life?*

He stepped towards the door at the head of the staircase that led to the garage. *Time to go.* The doorbell sang out again behind him, followed by the shave-and-a-haircut tattoo a neighbor might use.

He didn't pause this time, but grabbed the doorknob and turned it. A pop sounded from the front room. *What the . . .?* He turned toward the sound before he realized he'd stopped again. Tightness closed up the back of his throat. *Out of here. Now!*

He pushed the door open and stepped onto the stairway as a voice behind him called, "Stop! Hands above your head where I can see them. You're in my sights. One more step, and you're dead meat."

Roy dropped the bagged sandwich and stood still, his back to the voice. *Mulback's?* He listened—knees flexed slightly, weight centered on the balls of his feet—ready to move in any direction. He heard the chain on the front door jingle. He slowly lowered one hand toward his waist. Then, as the latch clicked open, he seized his gun, spun sideways back into the entry hall, and shot where he expected the officer to stand. The shot missed, punching out through the front wall to the right of the door. He cursed, but hoped it hit whoever was outside.

Benjamin had dropped to one knee. He returned fire, hitting Roy in the shoulder. The gun flew from Roy's hand as the impact rotated him around. He hit the wall and rebounded, barely keeping his feet beneath him.

One hand on his bloody shoulder, he raised the other and staggered a step before halting with a groan. He swayed as if his knees might buckle. "I'm hit!" he whined.

"Get that other hand up, too," Benjamin said with a snap.

He raised it haltingly, and began to turn toward the cop, bent partway over, whimpering with each breath. But the moment he faced the stairs, he darted through the open door and swung it shut behind him. He clattered down the flight toward the garage, fishing in a pocket for his keys.

A shot came through the door and zinged above his head. He heard the front door bounce open behind him as he ran, but the door he had closed earned him an extra second. A gunshot cracked as he reached the far side of the car and jerked open its door. He slithered halfway inside on his belly, keeping low to offer less of a target. His breath puffed.

He reached a swift hand up and hit the automatic opener to the garage, and then released the emergency break and put the car into neutral. Head still down, one hand on the dashboard and one on the bottom of the steering wheel, he braced his feet against the garage floor and pushed until the car rolled forward down the slight grade toward the steeper driveway. He jumped inside the vehicle, keeping low, and slipped the key into the ignition.

A second shot cracked as Benjamin splintered the windshields. Roy sat up and turned over the engine, already feeding the car gas as his eyes took a quick photo of the driveway. He ducked low again just before another bullet whizzed past. The car sprang forward.

A police cruiser screeched into the driveway, swerved sideways, and diagonally blocked Roy's exit from the garage. Ana jumped clear of the vehicle, pulled Alice out of the back seat behind her, and ran to the side. She drew her gun.

Head below the dashboard, unable to see, Roy pressed the accelerator, wild to escape the gunshots. With a shriek of tearing metal, his car smashed directly into the side of Anders's police car.

Two shots from Ana took out half of Roy's tires as insurance. Stunned by the crash and his gunshot wound, Roy offered no resistance when she pulled him from the car and cuffed him.

"The only place you're going today is to lock-up," Benjamin said, joining the couple. He called for transport.

With both the front and back doors open, officers moved through the old house, checking for other risks. Alice didn't wait for permission, but pushed inside, trying to locate her husband. Finding the door to the cellar stairs, she unlocked it, flipped on the light and started down. A grunt came to her ears, and she scuttled faster.

"Matthew!"

Anders growled. "Alice—watch out! Let me go first. There could be danger!"

She ignored him and continued down the stairs. At the bottom she saw the wet box, in a puddle of water, with its side forced ajar. Anders appeared beside her.

She saw him swing around, making sure the room was safe. Then he pulled a key out of his pocket, and touched her arm.

"Try this." He held it out and she grabbed it.

"Matthew! I'm here, sweetheart," Alice called out. She knelt by the box and tried the key in the exterior padlock. It yielded with a snap.

Using both hands, she wriggled the padlock back and forth in the hasp, which was under pressure from Matthew's efforts. Then it popped free, and the top of the lid sprang upward. She grabbed it and pushed it the rest of the way open. A shoe fell back into the box.

"Alice." Matthew's voice sounded scratchy. "You found me." He was lying on his back, his hands and one bare foot bleeding from scrapes. He wore the same clothes he had worn the day of the ransom, though his trousers were now stained around the crotch. The chain between his wrists had broken apart although his hands and feet still wore cuffs. He looked unwashed and unshaven, but he didn't seem beaten.

His eyes squinted in the light. He stared at her as if unsure whether she was another hallucination.

She jabbered at him. "It's me, sweetheart. The police figured out where you were. I didn't trust them, especially after the handoff. I thought they'd lose you, for certain. But they followed the kidnapper here and I followed them. You're safe now. I won't leave you. You can come home again."

She stepped one of her feet inside his box, and helped him sit up. "How badly are you hurt? Do you need a doctor?"

"I need water," he croaked.

"I'll get you some."

She turned and strode out of the box toward the stairs. Spotting the partial case of bottled water in a corner, she ripped one loose from the plastic wrapping, twisted off the lid, and handed him the container.

Matthew grasped it in both damaged hands and chugged down liquid in huge gulps, while water dribbled down from the corners of his mouth onto his shirt.

"Careful honey. Not too fast—it'll come back up. How long have you gone without water?"

He pried the bottle from his mouth, coughed and caught his breath, wiping his chin on his sleeve. "I'm not sure. What day is this?"

The poignant question overwhelmed Alice. In answer, she sat on the edge of the box beside him and began to cry, speaking his name, stroking his face and squeezing one of his hands like she'd never let go.

Anders left them together there.

Epilogue

When Anders arrived at the pottery studio, he found Marca already cleaned up and waiting for him, her now-booted foot propped on a stool, her clay-covered clothes tucked into a canvas bag. Her smile was broad.

"Look!" She pointed to her foot. "They gave me a boot. No more crutches." She waved her arms in the air. "I can walk now! But probably no dancing quite yet."

"Tell me if I don't cut you enough slack." He winked.

Marca giggled.

He laughed along with her friends, all familiar now. Lisa and Briana greeted him by name, as if he was an old friend, and he shook several hands. He had become far more than the chief investigator on their case. He was one of their family.

"Did you discover whose cremains were in the kiln?" asked Lisa, her brows pulled together.

"We think so. In Roy's house, in a corner of the attic, we found an empty cremation urn with a name inscribed on a metal plate attached to the front. Public records identified the man as Roy's uncle who passed away 20 years ago. The family kept his ashes all this time."

"So nobody was killed?" Briana asked.

"Not in the kiln, anyway. The bone chips, the fillings, and the screws fit with the remains being quite old. These days, the crematory mortician removes the metal and grinds the bone fragments. The older cremains hadn't had the modern treatment. So it looked like a murder-by-kiln, though it was not. Roy spread the cremains wide enough, in a reasonably human pattern, that they might have come from a burned body. He knew that would lead us to assume they were Matthew's."

"I'm glad the bad guy didn't get away with it," Quent said.

Anders shrugged. "He was smart, but not smart enough for Ana Nguyen, our criminalist. She compared the number of fillings and noted a missing leg-plate that indicated a staged murder."

"I'm relieved, actually," said Lisa. "I worried that some innocent person had been killed as a diversion from the real crime. No matter who was killed here, this place had been spoiled for me."

"Yes, I remember Marca sharing your theory with me after the potluck. It was a thoughtful one. And not so far from the truth."

"That the killing was a fake makes the studio feel safer again," she said.

"I'm glad. It's a special place," Anders said.

"Did I tell you? Anders got accolades from the police chief for solving the case," Marca said, and clapped her hands.

"All that means is that the older officers may quit calling me the new guy, if I'm lucky," Anders said with a grin. "But I missed some clues a more experienced detective would have found. I still have lots to learn."

"I told you I'm not a killer," Quent said.

"You're completely cleared," said Anders. "But I have to ask, why did you try to open the front door to this studio on the Wednesday and Thursday after you'd been asked to clear out of here?"

"To see if the lab was open yet. I rode over with my mom to her work, and then I walked back to check the door and get a Starbuck's latte each day. But on Friday, I went to the potluck instead, and Tim told us it would reopen on Saturday. So I stopped. But how did you know I came here?"

"A guard, Officer Landsbury, saw you on Wednesday and we took your fingerprints from the doorknob. And Roy Tenison, the bad guy, filled in as the Thursday guard. He took your picture turning the doorknob and made sure to tell me how suspicious you looked. Now I realize that he was trying to focus my attention on you as a suspect in order to keep us from considering him."

Anders turned to the room. "Thank you all for your help. It's rare that everyone cooperates with fingerprinting, DNA samples, and multiple questioning as willingly as you people. I appreciate the help you gave Marca as well." He smiled at her.

"We all help each other," she said. "I think of the potters in this studio as a family of choice."

"Did you hear the latest news?" Briana asked. "Matthew will lead the second half of our workshop next week. He had some trouble with flashbacks from his confinement, so I was surprised when he offered to come. He told Tim that he's glad that he's around to do it, and he's excited to share what he brought along for week two."

216 Sharman Badgett-Young

"All our pieces have been bisqued. Matthew says he can't wait to show us how to use his glazes." Ju-Mie grinned.

"Remember Lisa's Unicorn box?" Dave asked. "Now she can make one with attacking ninja monkeys and vampire cats on it as well."

"I'll get you for that." Lisa shook a fist at Dave.

Laughter erupted all around.

"I'm so excited, I want to do my happy dance. But I haven't dared dance in my boot yet," Marca said.

"Just because you're home now and in a walking cast doesn't mean that you can abuse your leg." Lisa gave Marca a stern look, and wagged her finger as if giving a mother-daughter lecture.

Marca giggled. "Well, mudpeople, I love you all, but I have a date." She glanced at Anders.

"Wait a few minutes longer," Anders said. "There's something in the car I need to grab. I'll be right back."

Marca looked at the others and shrugged as he left.

"Aren't you the lucky one, Marca. He's a looker," Kit said.

"Next time, though, I think you can find a date without having a car drive over your leg. That was extreme," Briana said.

"Who knows? My mother taught me that a guy who sympathizes with me is likely to ask me out," Marca smirked.

Several other potters teased her about her new romance. She giggled, and they laughed with her.

"Did I miss the punch line?" Anders asked as he set a tall item, wrapped in plastic, on the table.

He turned to Marca. "This isn't from me, you know. It wouldn't be here at all except for the care it got from our criminalist, Ana Nguyen."

Marca unwrapped the plastic. Her giant urn was only slightly drier than the last time she saw it, but looked otherwise unchanged.

"Ana made a cast of the fist print using flexible liquid latex, so it wouldn't cause much damage. She squirted it down with water each day and rewrapped it so it would remain moist for you," Anders said.

Marca examined the pot and fingered the clay. "Just right. I'll trim it next time I come in." She raised her hands over her head and clapped and turned once around in little steps, pivoting on her booted foot, as if she was the soloist of the moment in a Salsa circle. The others clapped along. "There's a happy dance for you," she laughed. "I'll do a better one the next time I see your criminalist, Anders."

"She'd love that," he said.

"You know, I think I'll leave that fist print in the urn. It has a history now—and is on the road to fame. Probably become quite valuable. At the least, it will always start an entertaining conversation." She grinned and rewrapped the pot. Lisa took it from her and set it back in the corner where it sat when the mystery began.

"Ready to go?" asked Anders, extending his hand to Marca.

"Let's," she smiled, and took it. He helped her stand and, still favoring her leg, they walked to the door. "Later all!" she called out, and heard parting words in return as she limped out of the studio.

When the pair got to the car, Anders held the door for Marca on the passenger's side, and gave her a hand in. He stood for a moment, smiling down at her.

"Not always, in police work, do we come up with this happy an ending," he said. Nobody died, after all, and you and Matthew will heal."

"You did great, Anders."

He leaned over and kissed her dark lips, a lingering kiss. "I hope you don't mind, but I've waited a long time to do that."

"Me too," she giggled. "Want to do it again?"

He did indeed.